WE MOVED IN SHADOW

Travelling north by car, David Stanmore makes a fateful stopover at a pub, where a thief steals a woman's handbag and then disappears. The distraught woman tells Stanmore that she had been on a covert mission for her employer to meet his friend in York, who was to give her information on the location of a hidden Nazi hoard of treasure. Her handbag had contained a visiting card that was to serve as her introduction. Stanmore agrees to take her in pursuit — and plunges into a nightmare world of death . . .

DENIS HUGHES

WE MOVED
IN SHADOW

Complete and Unabridged

LINFORD
Leicester

First published in Great Britain

First Linford Edition
published 2018

A catalogue record for this book is available
from the British Library.

ISBN 978–1–4448–3732–2

Published by
F. A. Thorpe (Publishing)
Anstey, Leicestershire

Set by Words & Graphics Ltd.
Anstey, Leicestershire
Printed and bound in Great Britain by
T. J. International Ltd., Padstow, Cornwall

This book is printed on acid-free paper

1

The long sweeping spine of the Great North Road unfolded ahead in an endless river of black rain-washed tarmac. The steady flick-flack of the screen wiper before my face beat its ceaseless rhythm on my brain as the lean low-flanked old Bentley fled on through the growing night.

Edging round curves or storming hills in my way, I took no heed of the pelting rain. I barely noticed the speed-blurred hedges or marching telegraph poles at my side. My mind was full of the prospect of at last having a job of work to do and, after several months of enforced idleness, I found the idea pleasant. In fact I was as happy as a man has any right to be.

The car ran well and I made the most of it, driving fast with a light heart. Sometimes I wonder if I should have felt quite so happy had I had any inkling of the events that were even then crowding in on me. At that time I'd never heard of the elusive Christine. I hadn't come face to face with Rathmore, nor heard the sound of a tune in the dark hours that was to stand for peril and danger and sudden death. I hadn't seen the smile of murder in a man's cold eyes, nor known the wonder of a woman's love.

Newcastle was my destination; though had I known it then, I was not to reach it in the way I planned. And yet I fail to see how I could have foreseen these things. There was nothing sinister or mysterious in the steady throb of the exhaust, or the swish of the tyres on the streaming road; nor was there anything sinister in my own contented thoughts.

The town of Rodcaster lay ahead. Its dark sprawl came out to meet us, engulfing the Bentley in shadows like a cool black shroud enveloping some long-awaited corpse. The shuttered windows and smug-looking shop fronts with their blind glass eyes towered above and around, so that I was glad to reach the other side and pull up at the Tawny Owl for a final drink before closing time.

Pushing my way into the big low-ceilinged lounge, I returned the friendly greeting of Joe the barman as he caught sight of my figure through the press at the bar, and then we were chatting as I ordered a pint of mild-and-bitter. The place was full and busy, with barely half an hour to go before ten o'clock. I looked round at the crowd and found some amusement in trying to guess what each did for a living. Most of them were easy to place, but one customer had me stumped in the game I was playing. She sat at a table not far from the door and caught my attention for the very simple reason that not only was she alone, but was engrossed in reading a book. It struck me as curious that an attractive woman should be sitting there like that, but I came to the conclusion that she was probably waiting for someone.

The crowd weaved to and fro between us, at times blocking my view altogether. It must have been during one of these 'curtain falls' that the man came in. I know I hadn't noticed him before, but the next time I had a glimpse of the woman I saw her eyes fixed on his tall figure as it picked its way through the people. There was no sign of recognition on the part of either of them, but I was left with the odd impression that there was a trace of fear in her eyes when she saw him.

He sidled up behind her then, limping awkwardly as he thrust his way between a fat woman with a feather-decked hat and an obvious retired colonel. Something about his looks put me on my mettle, and a moment later his leg banged against the comer of the woman's table as he made to pass. I saw her start and jump to her feet as the glass at her elbow spilled its contents, and then he was bending over saying how sorry he was and would she forgive him. I couldn't hear the exact words, of course, but his expression and gestures were clear enough for a half-wit to read. She made some answer I could only guess, and, almost at once, without even waiting to make good the damage he had done, the man moved away from her side. That in itself was curious enough, but the thing that riveted my attention was the fact that instead of carrying on towards the bar, he turned back and headed for the door, covering the distance with surprising speed in spite of his ungainly limp.

That the whole manoeuvre was planned never entered my head at the time, and I put it down to plain bad manners; but when he reached the door and pushed it open, I had cause to think again. I saw something that nobody else appeared to have noticed. Partly concealed beneath the flap of his double-breasted jacket was the bulky handbag I had last seen on the chair beside the woman.

That one fleeting glimpse of shiny leather sent me into instantaneous action. I remember shouting above the heads of the crowd. Everyone immediately turned round to see what the fuss was about, but the loud hubbub of questions and answers drowned my warning. Forcing a way through the press of people, I made a beeline for the door, yelling to the woman as I passed. I saw her startled face when she heard my words, and the look of comprehension as she realised I was speaking the truth. I noticed, too, that there was something far more than understanding in her wide-eyed gaze as she sprang up from the table and ran after me. There was real fear there now, and not just a trace of it as I had imagined I saw before.

In a chaos of shouting, startled exclamations and one disjointed scream from the crowded room, I got the door open and flung myself through. It was pitch dark outside, and after the bright lights of the bar I was as good as blind. When at last I managed to get my bearings I found the courtyard deserted, but already growing faint on the night air I heard the sound of a fast receding car somewhere out on the road.

Uncertain what to do next, I paused irresolutely. Behind me there was a faint noise, and then the woman herself was standing beside me.

'He's gone,' I said flatly. I tried to make up my mind whether the car I could hear was heading north or south. There was no indication, but suddenly the woman gripped my arm fiercely, pointing to where a lamp on the wall threw pools of light across the soaking cobbles of the yard. In the centre of the patch of radiance lay a small black object.

'My bag!' she gasped, and letting go of my sleeve ran towards it. For an instant I watched her before following. As I ran up, I saw her flick it open and rummage through the contents with frantic haste. Just as I came up beside her, she looked up from her search. There was no need to ask if anything was wrong. I could see it at a glance.

'It's gone!' she whispered fearfully, almost as if she was speaking to herself.

'What's gone?' I asked. She started at the words, suddenly aware of my presence. Her face was miserable, strangely drawn and lined, where before it had been faultless. For a split second she gazed at me with a frightened stare, and then, to my amazement I saw two large tears well up in the deep brown eyes.

'Here, steady!' I said, wondering what to do. 'Have you lost something valuable? Is there anything I can do to help?'

'It's too late.' Her words were toneless and half stifled. 'I was tricked, and now it's too late. Oh, what shall I do?'

I took her by the arm and gently led her back to the door of the lounge. 'If you told me what you were talking about,' I said, 'I might be able to make some suggestion. You're speaking in riddles at the moment.'

She made no attempt to answer my question, but when we reached the door of the room again she pulled up short and faced me. 'Which way were you going when you stopped here?' she asked in an urgent tone of voice. The rain beat down on our heads in a steady drenching torrent.

'North,' I told her.

'As far as York?'

'As far as Newcastle. Why? Can I give you a lift?'

'That man was going to York,' she said surprisingly. 'Could you catch him? Or get there first?' Her voice was eager now. 'What's your car?'

'Bentley,' I answered with a tingle of excitement. 'Come on; you can tell me all about it as we go.'

We were running then, splashing across the uneven cobbles towards the car. A little breathlessly, she clambered in and I pressed the starter. In a wide mud-slinging arc, I flung the big motor round the yard and through the low bowed arch that bored like a tunnel to the road outside.

'It's a good straight run,' I said, raising my voice above the roar of the engine. 'He can't have more than five minutes' start. Unless he's got a first-class car, we'll catch him. Now do you mind telling me what this is all about? I gather he stole something from your bag — something pretty important.'

'He stole a man's life!' The words were so low I could scarcely hear them, but the shock of them almost made me swerve.

'What!' I gasped.

'Look,' she said. 'You'd better turn back. I've no right to drag you into this — it's too dangerous. I'm sorry I took advantage of you as I did. Please stop.'

'Don't talk rubbish!' I replied. 'I'm the one to judge if it's too dangerous. Anyhow, I've been bored for long enough since the war ended. I need a little stimulating!'

I grinned into the darkness, but the woman remained deadly serious. Her eyes were fixed on the road ahead, unseeing and frightened; her expression grave and troubled. In silence she hunched forward. The road came racing towards us as I pushed the speed even higher. What was I sticking my head into? I wondered. She talked in a way that was calculated to scare the daylights out of anyone. But this was England. I couldn't understand it, and concentrated instead on covering ground as quickly as possible. If my self-chosen task was to overtake a car in front, then I would do my level best to achieve it, but I was frankly curious at the same time.

'Hadn't you better tell me a little more?' I suggested gently. The question brought her back from her thoughts. She half-turned to face me in the darkness. Without speaking, she took a packet of cigarettes from her bag and lit one, cupping the flame of her lighter against the storm of wind as we tore on through the night.

'I could do with one of those,' I said.

My hands were full, and she lit it for me. Sinking back into her seat again, she sat still gazing ahead, a small, attractive, worried little figure in the shadows. I sensed her nearness rather than saw it. She was obviously trying to make up her mind about something, and I left her to it, knowing that sooner or later she must break the silence.

The rain thinned and finally stopped, but the spinning wheels flayed up a plume of spray on either side. The road was dark and wide and clear. I found my blood racing in my veins, tingling in rhythm to the defiant roar of the exhaust and the throb of the motor. My thoughts were in a whirl, but I wouldn't have changed that moment for anything. Here beside me, thrown into my life by an unreadable Fate, was a woman who gave me plenty to think about, interesting me beyond a natural desire to know her. If on top of that — as she clearly hinted — I was going to find myself in danger, it only served to add spice to the whole somewhat fantastic situation.

Presently she tossed her half-smoked

cigarette over the side and sat up straight, peering at my face in the gloom.

'If you get to York before that other man,' she began, 'you'll probably save someone's life. There's much more to it than that, but I can't tell you what it is — yet. Will you trust me?'

I considered her words for a moment. Obviously I was on tricky ground, and yet I could hardly imagine my passenger as being a crook of any kind. She was certainly not going to tell me more than she thought was good for me to know, but the reason behind her reticence I could not guess.

'What happens when we reach York?' I asked at last.

She didn't answer immediately, and I entertained hopes that she was making up her mind to tell me more. When at length she did speak, however, her voice was flat and discouraging.

'You can forget you ever saw me.'

'I might not want to,' I pointed out quietly.

'I hope you do, anyway.' There seemed to be a faint hint of bitterness or regret in her voice. I couldn't be sure, and for the moment kept quiet, then: 'Are you a criminal?' I sprang the question on her suddenly, but whatever I expected to gain from it was lost in a deep-throated roar behind us as a great rakish Mercedes pulled out to pass.

What speed it was doing I don't know, but the Bentley was travelling at something over seventy at the time, so it must have been moving. I remember feeling surprised as the long bonnet crept alongside and slid in front. For a space of perhaps ten seconds the two cars were level, and then something happened that made my nerves go taut like overstrung piano wire. Through the slit at the base of the side-curtain of the passenger side of the Mercedes came a gloved hand, and firmly held in the dark fingers was the unmistakable shape of a heavy snub-nosed automatic.

What followed is still somewhat hazy in my memory, but I became suddenly and uncomfortably aware of an ice-cold prickle of fear at the nape of my neck as I realised the gun was pointing directly towards me. Instinctively I rammed my foot down on the brake pedal and reached for the handbrake. Probably that action saved our lives. I don't know for certain, but I'm pretty sure, for, had I been hit when he fired, nothing could have prevented us from being smashed to pieces at the speed we were going.

At the same instant as the Mercedes leapt ahead like an unleashed greyhound, I saw from the corner of my eye a vivid little spurt of flame from the automatic; and then with a sickening lurch, the Bentley went into a slide with one of its front tyres burst.

For an endless nightmare of terrifying seconds, I fought to hold the skidding car and straighten out. The wet surface of the road did little to help me, and snaking madly despite my efforts, we slewed diagonally across towards the opposite side of the road. At the last moment I regained control and pulled the wheel hard over to avert disaster. With a crash that shook the wind from my body and threw the woman on top of me, the tail whipped round like an angry shark and struck the bank, bringing a shower of torn-up earth and stones tumbling about us.

Bad as it was, however, the shock of collision had brought the car to a standstill, and a little shakily I climbed down to see what damage had been done. Even before my feet touched the ground, the woman was struggling from her seat to stand beside me on the road. Of the Mercedes there was no sign, but when I switched off my own motor I could distinguish the thunder of its exhaust now faint and muted by distance.

'That was rather too near for my liking!' I said grimly. 'Were those gentry any friends of yours, by the way?'

She gave me a frightened look, and I saw that her face was very white and set. 'I suppose,' I added in a more kindly tone, 'they were something to do with your handbag being stolen?'

'Yes, I think so. They must have let us get in front, then tried to make sure we couldn't follow them.' Her reply was hesitant, as if she was uncertain of herself or the ground she trod. 'Oh, what can I possibly say?' she went on. 'It's all my fault, and now they've beaten me and smashed your car up into the bargain.' She looked so sorry for herself that I couldn't help smiling.

'I think the car's all right,' I said, after a hasty look round. 'I shouldn't worry about that.' The back was caked with mud and grass, but beyond the burst tyre and a buckled rear wing there appeared to be no other damage of a serious nature.

'If you'll help me change this wheel, we'll carry on,' I said. 'You still want to go to York, I take it?'

She nodded dumbly, then: 'Yes, please, but we'll be too late now, I'm afraid. I must go, though, but I feel terrible about what happened just then.'

'Forget it,' I said. 'You wouldn't have had time to feel bad about it if that bullet had hit me instead of this tyre. As it turned out, we were damned lucky to get away with it so lightly.'

I got the jack from the tool box in the tonneau, talking as I set to work. 'Look,' I said patiently 'in spite of what I've just preached, I do feel that you owe me a fuller explanation than you've so far given me. I don't mind a joke, but to have people shooting at me with intent to kill is going a bit too far for my liking.'

For a time she made no attempt to reply, and I could tell she was having some kind of emotional battle inside. As I got the front wheel off and slipped the spare into place on the hub, she began speaking.

'I don't know who you are or anything about you,' she said. 'But as you say, I do owe you something, and you've been very good to give me a lift like this. For what has happened, I can only say how really sorry I am, and I swear I should never have allowed you to have me with you if I'd thought for a moment they had the nerve to try anything like that attack.'

'Go on,' I urged quietly. 'I'll take all that as read. Just tell me what sort of madhouse I've walked into — I'm interested! Aid besides . . . I'd like to help you if I can. I think I'd better introduce myself before we go any further; my name's David Stanmore. What's yours?'

'Carol Marney,' she replied with a faint smile, then quickly went on with her story. 'I had an appointment to meet a man in York tonight for the purpose of getting some information from him. At the last moment before I set out from London, I received a phone message telling me that he would meet me instead at the Tawny Owl. Not for a moment did I suspect anything. I'd never seen the man, and he didn't know me from Adam, so the voice on the telephone meant nothing to me at the time. Now, of course, I can see it all quite plainly. I was tricked in the simplest possible manner, and this is the result. Those men in the car that went past took my only means of identification out of my bag. I had a visiting card that was to have been our introduction. Now that they have it, it means they'll get there first and find out what this man was supposed to pass on to me.'

'You're not being very explicit,' I pointed out as I used a copper hammer on the wheel nut. 'What was this mysterious man in York supposed to tell you? And why should the gentry in the Mercedes be so anxious to get there first?'

'But don't you see . . . ?' she began.

'No, I don't,' I cut in a little sharply. 'I wish to heaven you'd start from the beginning and tell me the whole yarn, if you want any help from me — and it's perfectly clear from everything I've seen up to date that you need looking after pretty badly — you'll have to trust me and make a clean breast of it. I asked you some time ago if you were a criminal. Before we go into things more deeply, please answer that question. If you are, I shan't do anything about it, but I would like to know what I'm up against, and who my partner in crime is.' I grinned at her where she stood in the glare of the headlights.

The vivid beam struck her features slantwise, making the lovely face a medley of harsh black shadow and ivory highlights. She moved aside again and the contours softened. I liked them better that way.

'I must admit,' I said reflectively, 'you don't look like my idea of a crook, but

19

one never knows.'

The wheel was securely in place by now, and we were ready to take the road again. I straightened up. 'Come on,' I said. 'Get in, and talk fast. I want to know a whole lot of things.'

In the light of the headlamps, I suddenly saw that she was smiling at me. I grinned back. 'What's the joke?' I asked.

'No joke, really,' she replied. 'I was rather amused to think you thought I might be a crook — it was quite a novel experience. I'm not, though, so you can rest assured on that score, but . . . ' She stopped uncertainly, then: 'Oh, it's all so difficult. You see, although I'm no more a crook than you are, I am working outside the law.' She stopped again, and watched me intently to see the result of her words. Whatever she saw must have reassured her, because a moment later, as we scrambled into the car and I backed away from the bank and started off down the road, she went on: 'You're not shocked or surprised?'

I shook my head. 'No,' I answered. 'Why should I be? It's quite obvious that you're up to something, and if it was all perfectly legal there wouldn't have been that recent little exhibition of gun-play. However much I may deplore such fun and games, I now bear a personal grudge against the man who tried to rub me out. In view of that, I'm prepared to wink at whatever it is that's going on and try to get my own back. Just go on and tell me more; I'm listening with both ears.'

We were travelling fast again, and the car appeared to be none the worse for our slight accident.

'Yes,' she said. 'I see what you mean. To be quite frank, I do need your help now — if you still want to give it, that is — and I'll have to trust you with all I know myself.' She paused and stole a glance at my shadowed face as I jockeyed the Bentley through a long curve. Her next words were quiet yet forceful. They gave me a spine-tingling thrill and made my pulse race faster.

'I'm looking for a large cache of Nazi money,' she said. There was a simple sincerity about the way she spoke that took the sting of absurdity from her announcement, so that I found myself accepting it in the manner she intended.

'During the war,' she continued, 'as you probably know already, there were quite a number of enemy agents in this country. In order to pay them, the German espionage organisation here had to have ready funds on which to draw. There were several sources, one of which was money brought into the country from outside, while another was through a set of people who acted as fences for specially selected criminals operating here. In those and other ways, they eventually amassed a vast hoard that is still hidden somewhere in this country.'

'How do you know all this?' I asked. 'Are you a secret service agent or something?'

'No. I'm secretary to a businessman in London named Paul Antoine — he's French. That's how I come into it.'

'I still don't see the connection,' I said. 'But go on.'

'This is what he told me when he sent me on the trip. Some years ago he was the victim of a pretty big robbery, and the things he lost have never been traced. Two days back, someone wrote him a letter saying that if he would send a contact to meet the writer, he would learn where his valuables were. The writer of the letter went on to say that he himself had once been a member of the Armée de Resistance, and was now in England engaged on secret liaison work. Knowledge of the whereabouts of Antoine's valuables — included in the cache I mentioned, as well as a lot of other stuff — had come into his possession. Being a somewhat unscrupulous man, he was prepared to sell his knowledge.'

'Sounds a pleasant piece of work!' I commented acidly. 'But look here, what about the man who stole your handbag and took that pot shot at me? Where did he materialise from?'

She didn't seem so sure of herself at that, but after a moment's hesitation, continued: 'I can't tell you exactly, but in his letter, this Frenchman hinted that there were others interested in the secret, and that he had to be careful how he acted — hence the air of mystery that surrounded my visit to York.'

'You mean it's a case of the person who presents that visiting card being accepted as your employer's agent and therefore entitled to learn the secret, is that it?'

'More or less. Of course, they'd have to pay him for it, just as my chief would have had to do. What I'm afraid of now is that they may go further than simply take his information. I'm scared that they'll kill him so that he can't pass it on to anyone else.'

I considered all she told me for some time before saying anything. That I was sticking my neck out and asking for trouble with a vengeance I had no doubt, but somehow the thought failed to weigh very heavily against my decision to carry on.

2

'You know this Frenchman's address?' I asked. Already the outskirts of York were beginning to press in around us, crowding down on the road like a clogging welter of groping limbs.

She fumbled in her bag and produced a scrap of paper. Reaching across to the dash-lamp, she switched it on and read aloud the name of a street. Neither of us had much idea where it was, but from my previous experience of the city, I had a vague notion that it lay somewhere north of the old cathedral.

'Couldn't we ask someone?' she wanted to know.

'We could,' I agreed, 'but I'd rather not attract too much attention if it can be helped. Suppose there's any trouble when we get there — or that it's happened already? The fact that we'd been asking our way at this time of night would sure to be remembered by somebody or other.

No,' I pointed out, 'it's too big a risk to take. Be much safer if we can find it on our own.'

She nodded understandingly. 'Yes,' she admitted. 'You're right. I'm glad I'm not alone — I don't seem to be cut out for this sort of thing.'

'You're not doing too badly so far.' I grinned as we edged in towards the centre of the city. 'What do you expect to find when we get to this man's house?'

'I don't know. I'm a little scared about the whole business now.'

'I'll be with you,' I said cheerfully, though I wasn't sure that my presence would make a lot of difference. However, I had no intention of being left out of anything from then on; and if there was any likelihood of trouble in York that night, I meant to be in on it.

'Keep your eyes skinned for that Mercedes,' I told her. 'We don't want that sneaking up on us again. I've developed quite a healthy dislike for the owner, whoever he is.'

We motored on through the sleeping town. I drove quite slowly now as our eyes searched every corner for the street name we wanted. It was Carol who saw it first, and I put my foot to the brake with a feeling of excitement. Here, then, I thought, was to begin the second phase of our strange adventure.

It was a mean enough setting in all conscience. The street was narrow, little better than an alley leading off one of the less prosperous business thoroughfares to the north of the city. Half the lamps were out, and long black shadows stretched like streamers of crepe across the pavement. It looked damp. It smelt damp. With a beating heart, I brought the car to a standstill close by the entrance.

As far as I could see, the whole place was deserted. Not a living soul stirred down its murky length. Almost might it have been a place of the dead. Somehow the simile gave me little comfort.

'What number is the house?' I asked.

'Twenty-two,' came her hushed reply. We climbed down and began walking through the shadows. An occasional patch of washed-out lamplight threw muddy puddles into glittering relief. A cat with great green eyes sought safety behind a refuse bin. The baleful hiss of its disapproval caused us both to start guiltily. Somehow I found the woman's arm through mine, her fingers gripping me tightly beneath my sleeve.

'Here we are,' I breathed. 'What now, I wonder?'

'He said to walk straight in,' she said. 'Ground floor flat.'

I looked at the door distastefully. It was small, flush with the pavement, and sketchily covered with badly blistered paint. One blind window leered at us from beside it. No glimmer of light showed either from the door or the window. The upper storey was also in darkness. Complete silence gave it an atmosphere of unutterable gloom and foreboding. I began to hate the place.

'We'd better try then,' I said quietly. 'Here goes.'

Pulling a torch from my pocket, I put a hand to the door knob and turned it. With a faintly protesting rattle it gave, and the door opened inwards. For an instant I stood still. An overpowering reek of stale, greasy cooking wafted towards us from the black maw of the interior. On the right side of the cramped passage was a single door.

'There's your ground floor flat,' I murmured a little grimly. 'Healthy-looking place, isn't it? Come on. Maybe your friend's asleep, or given you up for lost.'

'No friend of mine,' she breathed.

I took a step inside and made for the door on the right. All my senses revolted at the atmosphere. I felt keyed up to a pitch that was dangerous. If something had suddenly made a loud noise, I think I should have turned and run. It wasn't a pleasant thought, nor for that matter was it a pleasant place.

The door opened with a crack that sounded as sharp as a rifle shot in the eerie stillness. 'Hell,' I thought, cursing myself for a fool, 'I'm getting jumpy.' I could hear Carol behind me breathing hard, and then we were inside the room.

Black as a cavern, the darkness flooded over us. I shone the beam of the torch from side to side. The only furniture was a rickety tea-stained table and a tumbled, dirty-looking bed. The floor was covered with scraps and bits of rubbish. Faded paper hung from the walls in dank festoons.

'Nothing here,' I muttered. I felt strangely disappointed. 'You're sure this is the right address?'

'It's the only one I've got. He must have gone, or . . . or been taken away.'

I moved further inside and began examining the room more carefully.

'Maybe he left a message or something,' I suggested hopefully. We were over by the window when I spoke, and I was peering at the surface of the wall in search of anything that might have been written on it. The table was bare; the air was thick. I suddenly realised that probably the window hadn't been opened for weeks. It smelt that way. But there was something else, too, that made me think. On the narrow sill of the frame was a fresh-looking cigarette end. I put it to my nose and sniffed.

'Someone was here not long ago,' I said in a low voice. 'This is almost warm.'

'Then that can only mean they've already been and got what they want.' There was dread in her voice.

The atmosphere wasn't quite so oppressive now, though certainly Carol didn't share my feelings on that score. I wasn't whispering quite so low as before. She was still very close against me, fearful of being left alone. I couldn't blame her for that. For a second or two I stood, uncertain of what to do next. It was during that moment of utter silence that we heard it. It was nothing more than a thin, little gurgling whisper of sound, but it was quite enough to make my companion clutch hold of me and hang on as if a fiend had brushed past her face. I heard her gasp and catch her breath. I felt my scalp crawl icily as I slid an arm round her slim waist and drew her close.

'Mice!' I whispered as lightly as I could; but the trouble was that we both knew it was not mice. 'Steady,' I breathed. I disengaged her nervous fingers from my coat and took a step forward in the direction of the bed. The sound had come from underneath it.

Stooping down, I shone the torch. Hunched up against the wall, right at the back of the bed, was the body of a man. From under his coat and reaching almost to my feet was a narrow, sinuous river of crimson that I knew could only be blood.

3

For long dragging seconds, I remained motionless, crouching there with the sharp beam of the flash-lamp reaching out in front towards that ominous shape that had once been a man, living and breathing like myself.

It was Carol who shattered the spell and woke me to reality. I felt the grip of her fingers and heard her sudden intake of breath as she realised what I was looking at. I stood up and shifted the torch a little.

'Your Frenchman!' I whispered. 'Help me shove the bed out of the way. He may have something useful in his pockets.'

Between us, we pulled the rough bed away from the wall and clear of the body. I bent down to examine him, and as I did so found myself looking into a pair of eyes that burned hotly in the glimmer of light. They were small and close-set, mean and distrustful.

'Good Lord!' I gasped. 'He's not dead!' I pulled a flask from my pocket and forced the cold, hard rim between his teeth. 'Try to swallow some of this,' I urged. 'Tell us what happened.' He coughed horribly then, gouts of dark red blood flecking the thin white lips. Mixed with the pain in the hard, drawn face was suspicion and something like hate.

'Can't we do anything?' Carol asked.

I shook my head. 'Too risky to move him. Look.' Wordlessly I pointed. From the right side of his chest showed the long curved handle of a knife. Every time he drew a tortured breath, there came a little gurgling noise from around it. For a moment I crouched where I was, simply watching his face. It wasn't pretty. Carol came closer. I knew she was fighting against fear in her determination to learn the secret that had caught us both in its toils. One man, I thought grimly, was already dying because of it. How many more would it take before Death was satisfied? I tried to keep my mind clear, but found it difficult.

'You're Francois Gaston, aren't you?'

Carol's question was low and barely audible, but it had an effect on the dying man. He moved his head slightly, peering towards her face beyond the circle of light. I shifted the torch a little so that it revealed her more clearly. The travesty of a grin flickered for an instant across his lips, but there was no sign of recognition in his eyes.

'I've come from M'sieu Antoine,' she went on. 'I was tricked, or I'd have been here hours ago.'

His mouth began to move, striving to form words. At last they came, slow and indistinct. I bent my head to catch what syllables I could.

'Coolis beat you to it,' he muttered. 'I didn't know then, but I do now. They know where it is now, but the fools wouldn't wait. You'll never find it unless . . . ' He stopped, coughing violently. When the spasm was past, his eyes were dim and glazed, half-open, almost blind. I thought he was finished, but after a moment he began again. His voice was weaker now; the words even more disjointed.

'I wanted Christine to have the sapphire ring. Old Antoine knew. Now it's too late. You might get it if you're lucky.' He paused, fighting for breath. I think he knew the sands were running out. Desperately he hurried on: 'Go to Frigate's Hard. Whatever you do, be careful of Lili Marlene. And . . . and don't . . . forget . . . the Orange . . . Death . . . '

Vainly I tried to hear more, but it was gone. In a slurring jumble of sounds his head fell back, and I knew that anything I did would be useless. Francois Gaston, renegade Frenchman, late of the world-famed Armée de Resistance, was dead.

I stood up with Carol beside me. I felt tired and slightly sick. Whatever the man might have been in life, he had died hard and horribly.

'What now?' I muttered half to myself. I could feel the warmth of Carol's body at my side. I didn't want to waste time. Gaston must be searched in case there was anything to learn from the contents of his clothes. We knew little enough as it was. I dropped on my knee again. My nerves were on edge, but I succeeded in forcing down the feeling of revulsion inside me.

His clothes were ragged and dirty, little better than a tramp's. All I found was the visiting card that presumably was the one stolen from my companion's handbag at the Tawny Owl. Nothing else came to light. We were left hanging precariously to the thin end of knowledge with only the scantiest clues in our possession. A few words to guide us; hardly more than veiled threats of danger; the one single name of a place: Frigate's Hard. I put a hand to my head in bewilderment.

'Come on,' I breathed. 'This is no place for us. It'll be too unhealthy if anyone finds us here.'

Her long, cold fingers found mine in the darkness. Together we crept from the room and down the passage to the front door. Outside, the alley was as dark and depressing as it had ever been. With an immense feeling of relief, I saw the lean shape of the Bentley standing not twenty yards away, just as we had left it. There was something refreshingly sane about the sight of its gaunt, mud-streaked flanks. We hurried on and clambered aboard a little breathlessly. I felt I wanted time to think and sort things out into some kind of order.

No further words were spoken between us till we were clear of the place and I turned the car into the canopied fore-court of the railway station. I thought we should be able to linger there and talk things over without arousing too much attention. There was a train due in from London in half an hour, and we could easily pretend to be waiting for it if anyone became curious. I pulled up and lit a cigarette, passing the packet across to Carol. For several seconds, neither of us said a word. I was hopelessly puzzled, and she, I think, was badly shaken by what we had seen and heard.

'Oughtn't we to go to the police and tell them everything?' she said at last.

'And get ourselves involved, in endless questions? I think we'd do better to keep what we know to ourselves for the moment. I know it's a very illegal way of looking at things, but unless we act on what we know immediately, we shall lose all trace of this precious treasure. Besides,' I added, 'I still have a count to settle with the merchant who took that shot at me.'

'We'll probably both end up in prison,' she said.

I grinned. 'They tell me the second division isn't too bad these days!' I felt I wanted some light relief in the nightmare into which we'd both been flung. 'Seriously, though,' I went on, 'what do we know? There's far too much about tins affair I don't understand. Can you add anything? Or are you just as much in the dark as I am, after Gaston's riddles? Who's Christine, for instance? And Lili Marlene? Where's Frigate's Hard? And last, but not least, what on earth is Orange Death? Frankly I'm stumped. Unless you can guide me a little, I fail to see what to do next.'

She didn't say anything at that, and I leaned back, peering up at the green steel arches that spread above our heads. I couldn't forget the dead man back there in the sordid hovel we'd left. It all seemed so unreal. Not for the first time had I seen death. I'd seen it on the shell-torn beaches of France; on the sun-tanned hills of Italy. But not like that. Then it had come with the vicious nickel-clad lead of kicking Spandaus, or the diabolical shriek of eighty-eights. This was a very different matter.

Suddenly I found myself hating the man who had done it. Gaston might have been bad, bad right through for all I knew, but surely there was no need to kill him so ruthlessly. Apparently, too, he must have had some human emotions in his make-up. That odd reference to Christine and a sapphire ring was proof of that. Who the devil did he mean? That was something I simply had to find out. Was it reasonable to suppose that among the fabulous treasure we sought was an heirloom the man had intended should go to his wife, or sweetheart, or mistress, or . . . daughter? I didn't know. I didn't even know if he had any relatives at all. I felt like a blind man whose stick has been stolen.

Carol made a movement, stretching her legs out under the dash. Slight as it was, it stirred me to wakefulness. 'We'll have breakfast in London,' I said, suddenly making up my mind. 'Your M'sieu Antoine shall help in the problem. After all, it's his own.'

'London!' she gasped.

I nodded and lit another cigarette. 'Make yourself comfortable, Carol. It's a long drive, but we ought to be there not later than eight at the latest.' I got down and approached a policeman at the entrance of the booking office.

'Where's the nearest all-night filling station, officer?' I asked politely. I had a funny feeling that he might remember me again if the need arose, but he gave the information readily enough, and with a word of thanks I turned back to the car.

York lay sleeping as we left it, outwardly as peaceful as when we had arrived, but both of us knew now that among its myriad people there was one who would never again rub the drowsiness of morning from his eyes. The thought depressed me, and I drove fast to lose it. Hedges, banks, streams and bridges raced up, whirled past and fell behind. I gave the Bentley all she wanted and revelled in it.

Somewhere close to Grantham, we stopped at a roadside coffee stall. Heavy goods lorries lined the road, their snub bonnets facing north and south. The main artery of England reached out in front and behind. Like little black corpuscles of a nation's life blood, the trucks thundered past in either direction. The wooden hut was close and damp, full of the reek of tobacco smoke and diesel oil from the lorries outside.

A flood of cheerful voices swept over us as we walked in. Men in greasy caps and oily overalls stood or sat on every side. Behind the enormous tea urn presided a fat young man with long dank hair that clung to his forehead in sweaty wisps. Two drivers in a far corner were playing dominoes, their heads bent forward as if nothing else in the world was of greater importance. I thought of the man in York.

'Tea or corfy?' asked the fat youth, wiping large hands on a grubby apron. I was hungry, rather tired, and very thirsty.

'One tea, one coffee, both without

sugar,' I answered after a brief consultation with Carol. 'We'd better have some of those sandwiches as well, I think.'

We made our way to a table and sat down against the wall. I felt relaxed and eager to be on the road again as soon as possible. For a while we ate and drank in silence. The swelling murmur of voices around us made me drowsy; so did the thick air. I tried to pick out scraps of conversation. You could if you listened carefully.

'Must a' bin doin' near an 'undred . . . '

'S'pose 'e didn't see it in time . . . '

'Yer should 'ave seen the mess, George . . . '

'I came by not 'arf an hour after . . . '

'Go on. Yer don't say.'

'Some young fool . . . '

Curiosity livened me up. I leaned over and touched the nearest man on the arm. 'What happened?' I wanted to know.

For a moment he eyed me doubtfully. Then: 'Some bloke in a racing Merc wrote hisseif orf a coupla mile down the road,' he said. 'Goin' south 'ell for leather and 'it the bank. Smashed to bits, 'e was.

Passed me earlier on, and I could have swore there were two men in it then, but I dunno now. They was clearin' the mess up when I come through, and I only saw one body meself. 'E'd 'ad it and no mistake.'

I didn't wait for any more. 'Come on,' I said to Carol. 'We'd better be moving on.'

I desperately wanted to see the wreckage of the Mercedes. It would be a coincidence, of course, but they're not a very common motor on the roads. Suppose it was the one that we had already met once that night? What would be the inference? I didn't know, but I wanted to find out.

There was no difficulty in locating the scene of the accident. A cluster of red lights stood at the side of the road, and as we drove up I made out the gaunt outline of a breakdown crane hoisting a mass of twisted metal clear of the road to swing it onto the verge. Great scars showed up on the asphalt where what was left of the Mercedes had torn itself along after striking the bank. We were close enough to see every detail, and even in its wrecked state the car needed no more than a second glance on my part to identify it with the one that had so nearly been the cause of my own death.

I didn't feel sorry or glad. I just looked at it dispassionately. Two men; one body. That was all the lorry driver had said he saw. Where was the other, then? Surely no man could live after a smash like that must have been. I brought the car to a standstill and got out, motioning Carol to stay where she was. The blue uniformed figure of a police patrol was directing operations at the breakdown lorry. I sidled up casually and stood beside him.

'Anyone hurt?' I asked with an assumption of idiocy. 'I'll do what I can to help if you like.'

He eyed me distastefully, obviously having a healthy dislike for morbid sightseers. 'You'd do better to be on your way if you don't mind, sir,' he replied. 'We've all the help we need, and you'd only be in the way.'

I stood and watched the crane, ignoring the hint for a moment. 'Made a bit of a mess of it, didn't they?' I said.

He nodded ponderously. 'There was only one man in it, luckily. He was killed outright.'

'That's funny. One of the drivers in the café down the road said he thought there were two of them. Must have made a mistake, I suppose.'

'Shouldn't be surprised, sir. Now, if you don't mind, I'd be glad if you'd move along. We don't want the road blocked up with cars. Got our hands full enough as it is.'

'Of course,' I replied quickly. 'Good night, Officer.'

'G'night, sir,' he answered shortly, and I knew very well he was only too pleased to see the back of me. I climbed into the Bentley and started off. There was no sense in lingering or causing suspicion by nosing around where we were far from welcome.

'That was the same car, wasn't it?' Carol's voice was small and intense.

'Yes,' I said. 'What's more, I've a hunch that there were two men in it when it cracked up. Nobody here thinks so, but that man in the café seemed pretty certain of himself, didn't he? I'm just wondering what it all means.'

'I think I can make a fair guess,' she said hesitantly. 'Suppose they were the men who killed Gaston. They got the secret from him and were on their way to Frigate's Hard, or wherever the treasure is. Then they have this smash, but one of them escapes; and as soon as he finds out that the other is dead, he just fades away, obviously not wanting to be hung up after the accident. I'm sure something like that must have happened.'

'You may be right,' I replied cautiously. 'If you are, it means that the second merchant is still in the game and well on his way again by now.' I paused, then: 'There's one good thing to come out of this. If, as we can safely assume, they were heading for Frigate's Hard, it seems clear that it must lie south of here. It's not much to work on, I know, but it does narrow the field to a certain extent.'

'Do we still go to London?'

'Yes, I think it'd be the wisest thing to do. We're simply wasting time groping round in the dark as it is. Antoine may

47

have something up his sleeve about which we know nothing. When he hears the yarn, he may feel inclined to tell us whatever it is, if anything. Surely, he must have known something about that man, Gaston. There must be some connection between them, or why should the Frenchman have taken the trouble to write to him and offer to tell where the cache is hidden? It stands to reason that there's more to it than we know. As far as I can see, Antoine is the only person who can help clear it up.'

I paused and asked her for a cigarette. The night tore by on either side as the long, undulating road swept past. Faintly gleaming stars showed through the jagged cloud-wrack high above. Beyond the narrow world of the silver headlamp beam, the darkness seemed to live and breathe. To the end of my days, I shall never forget that mad night drive from York to London.

'What's this fellow Antoine like?' I asked presently. It struck me that I knew hardly anything about either Carol beside me or the man she worked for. I knew her name, but no part of her history; and yet I liked her company, strange and hazardous as it had so far proved. I stole a glance at the dark silhouette of her finely chiselled features. The slightly parted lips were rich and warm; tiny white teeth gleamed out behind them. Her small nose was fractionally tilted; the deep brown eyes fixed away on infinite distance. The whole made a picture that stirred my blood, raising unexpected emotions inside me.

'Antoine!' I repeated, jogging her from the reverie in which she sat. 'Tell me about him.'

'Sorry,' she said with a little laugh. 'I was thinking.' She paused before going on. 'It's funny, but I can't tell you an awful lot about him. In spite of the fact that I've known him for several years, I still hardly know more than the bare details about his background. First of all he's a wine-importer, and quite a prosperous man. He's short and thick-set, with a funny little pointed beard just like a picture. He was married once, but I believe his wife died.'

'How did you come to meet him and work for him?'

'It dates back to 1941. My people were killed in a raid on London, and Antoine was close by when the house came down. I wasn't badly hurt myself, but he helped to pull me out and insisted on taking care of me afterwards. He was terribly kind and finally gave me a job as a sort of private secretary. I think he was sorry for me. I thought at first that he might have ulterior motives, but he's been nothing but goodness itself. I owe him an awful lot, really.'

'What age is he?'

'Fiftyish, I should say, though I'm not sure. That's more or less all I can tell you about him.'

'And I take it you'd never heard of this other man Gaston until he wrote to Antoine?'

She shook her darkly curling hair. 'Not a murmur. As far as I'm concerned, he just dropped out of the blue. M'sieur Antoine would have gone to keep the appointment himself, but had to attend an important conference yesterday and couldn't get away. That's why he asked me to do it. He trusts me implicitly in all his business affairs, and I'm certain he never expected it to end up the way it did.' She gave a little shudder and looked away at the flying road ahead.

For a while after that, we thundered on without speaking, my own mind busy with the scanty details we had so far gleaned. I barely noticed the country unfolding in front, nor the first faint tinge of red in the eastern sky. Dawn stole up on us in a pageant of crimson laced with blue; flamboyant banners of hazy vapour steamed across the heavens like fingers of light from another world. Almost before I realised it, the nascent sun came up to dress the fields and valleys in a mantle of shimmering gold. Another day had found us; the first full day I was to share with the woman beside me; a day of strange and puzzling events.

The morning promised fair, but the sunrise itself was red. Long afterwards, I was to remember the sinister warning it carried.

'Hungry?' I said cheerfully. The journey

was almost over now. I threaded my way towards Hampstead, where Carol told me Antoine lived.

'I think I could eat a horse!' she replied with a silvery laugh. Her eyes met mine, then suddenly grew serious. 'How are you going to explain yourself?' she asked. 'He'll want to know how you come into it, won't he?'

I shrugged my shoulders. 'Tell him the truth, I suppose. There's no other way, is there? Surely he can't object to my getting you out of trouble that he got you into — even if it was inadvertently. Anyhow, I'm far too deep in this thing now to be pushed out in a hurry. Besides,' I added with a smile, 'I find life very interesting at the moment.'

Her teeth flashed white as she laughed in the sunlight. 'I'm glad I met you,' she said. 'It's been exciting, hasn't it?'

'Almost too much so.' I couldn't forget that we'd smelt death that night. 'I only hope nobody connects us with York when they find Gaston's body.'

'It would be awkward, wouldn't it? Perhaps they won't find him for several days, and by then anything may have happened.'

'That's what I'm afraid of,' I retorted grimly. 'Anything.'

As I spoke the words, I swung the wheel over and turned in through the big wrought-iron gates of a substantial-looking house that stood well back in its own spacious grounds. 'He lives well by the look of it,' I commented. 'Nice place.'

'It's beautiful inside,' she answered as I drew up in front of the wide oak doors. We clambered down, stiff and tired after long hours on the road.

'Let's hope they've got eggs and bacon for breakfast.' I grinned. I put a hand to the bell push, but Carol stopped me.

'I have my own key,' she said.

A moment later we walked into a cool entrance hall. Glistening parquet flooring clicked hard and smooth beneath our feet. I found myself liking the place. It had a warm, friendly sort of welcome about it. My companion led me through to a long panelled room at the far end. Tall French windows opened out to the perfectly kept garden beyond, a lovely riot of terraces and rose trees. Despite the early hour, a log fire already blazed cosily in the deep-set hearth.

'Sit down and make yourself comfortable,' she told me. 'Antoine won't be up yet, but I'll see what I can do about some breakfast.'

'Don't be long,' I said, picking up a morning paper and choosing an armchair beside the fire. Gratefully I sank into its comforting arms and stretched my weary limbs. The door closed behind her, and I was alone.

How many seconds she was gone, I don't know, but suddenly she was standing before me again, her face alive with some emotion I could not read.

'What's the matter?' I gasped, starting up from my seat.

'Antoine!' she stammered. 'He's . . . he's dead!' The words choked into silence.

I sat down weakly in the chair beside me, stunned. There seemed nothing I could do or say at that moment. In the end I managed to open my mouth to speak, but before I could utter a word the door opened again and the figure of a beneficent-looking butler entered.

'Will you have breakfast in here or in the morning-room Miss Carol?' His tone was hushed and respectful; too much so for my liking.

She glanced up, a queer, haunted expression in her eyes. 'Oh, anywhere, Bulmers. I'm not . . . I'm not very hungry now.'

'Very good, miss. Will the gentleman require anything?'

'Yes, please,' I said. 'Bring me a double whisky.'

'Certainly, sir.' He turned to leave, but I halted him at the door. 'Just a moment,' I said quickly. 'I understand something has happened to M'sieu Antoine. Is he dead? I was to have seen him on urgent business.'

The man's eyebrows raised a fraction, but beyond that no tremor of emotion showed on his smooth, bland face. 'I was informed by phone an hour ago, sir, that the master died as the result of a motor accident during the night. It is a great blow to me, but I am afraid I can tell you nothing else. I believe the Grantham

Police have details of the accident should you require them.' He paused. 'And now if you will excuse me, sir.'

'Yes, of course,' I replied mechanically.

One fact was battling for recognition inside my brain. The Mercedes smash had taken place close to Grantham.

Carol and I sat still, facing one another across the hearthrug; the same incredible thought, the same dread, the same unanswerable question hammering itself continuously at the minds of both of us.

4

The soft-footed return of Bulmers loosened my tongue. With a warning glance at Carol, I addressed him as he set a decanter and syphon at my elbow.

'At what time did M'sieu Antoine leave yesterday?' I asked, trying not to put more than natural curiosity into my voice.

'He received a telephone message about seven o'clock in the evening, sir, and went out almost immediately. I asked him when I was to expect him back, and he told me it would probably not be until this morning.'

'I see.' And yet seeing was the last thing I did. The more I tried to understand, the deeper in the mire of ignorance I seemed to sink.

As soon as we were alone again, I stood up with a drink in my hand and looked down at Carol. She hadn't uttered a single word since her first startling announcement, and try as I would, I could make nothing of her subsequent silence or the expression that went with it. I had a queer feeling that something was being held back from me, and the idea irked me. After all, I argued, I'd thrown my hand in whole-heartedly enough in an attempt to solve her problems, and if I was not going to receive the full confidence and co-operation my gesture deserved, I wanted to know why.

'Have you told me *everything* you know about this affair?' I asked suddenly. 'It seems to me that there are a lot of things that don't fit, and I've a damn good mind to chuck it and tell the police what little I know. For one thing, there's already been one murder; and now, on top of that, this mysterious employer of yours has become very dead under circumstances which to my mind call for investigation.'

I stopped to see what effect, if any, my words had had on her. Her face was a little pale, but the eyes were honest enough as she returned my frankly suspicious stare. Before answering my challenge, however, she took a cigarette from the engraved silver box beside her, offering it to me as she did so. Automatically, I accepted one for myself and sat down again.

'We don't know for sure that Antoine *was* killed in that Mercedes wreck,' she pointed out, ignoring the rest of my remarks.

'It's too big a coincidence to overlook,' I retorted. 'The odds are all in favour of that being the way he died, if you ask me. Frankly I don't like it, and I don't mind saying so. If my guess is right, it was Antoine in the Mercedes, and it therefore follows that either he himself or someone with him took that shot at me last night and tried to rub us out. I say *us* because whoever did it must have known you were in the car with me; and seeing that until then I'd never come into the picture at all, it strikes me that it was really you they wanted out of the way more than me. The fact that I should have been killed as well if we'd had a proper smash apparently meant nothing to them.'

'You're arguing on quite sound lines,' she admitted. 'But has it struck you that there's something very wrong with your theory? Why should Antoine have had a hand in it?'

'How do you mean?' I demanded. 'I should say he had a big hand in it!'

She looked at me defiantly. 'If he never intended me to reach York and keep that appointment with Gaston, why did he go to the trouble of trying to stop me in such a clumsy manner? Surely all he had to do was simply not send me in the first place. You must admit that it just doesn't tie up, does it?'

I grunted. What she said was true, of course. I'd seen it coming from the start, but I had to find some way round. 'I don't believe he told you the truth when he sent you,' I said. 'Did you actually see that letter he was supposed to receive from Gaston?'

She shook her head doubtfully. 'No, I didn't. Antoine simply called me in and gave me instructions about meeting him. He told me exactly what I've already told you about the Frenchman I was to contact, and the cache, and . . . everything else. That's honestly all I know.'

I'd have staked my life that she was telling the truth. Seeing that there was nothing definite against the assumption, I had to accept it.

'I'd like to see that letter,' I said at last. 'Could we find it, do you think? It wouldn't do any harm to read it for ourselves, and it might tell a very different story to what we've been led to believe. It seems to me that your precious Antoine was a tricky customer, though how or why I can't imagine.'

She stood up at that and moved to the door. 'Yes, I think we're justified in doing that,' she said. Her parting words had a hint of eagerness about them, and I felt a slight prickle of expectation as I waited for her return.

Until then I'd forgotten all about breakfast in the tangle of mystery in which I was moving, but the sudden arrival of the archdeacon-like figure of Bulmers brought me back to the remembrance of hunger. Gratefully I followed him to another room and found myself confronted with an appetising array of bacon and eggs and steaming coffee laid on a table before the window. Without more ado I set about eating, and not till I was halfway through the meal did Carol come in to join me.

I could see at a glance that something was in the wind as soon as she entered. Her face was grave and worried, and her first words did little to allay my fears that she had found further problems in her search for clues.

'I've unearthed more than I bargained for,' she said. 'You'd better come and have a look for yourself.'

Together we walked through the hall and up a flight of stairs that would have graced a palace. The treads were wide and shallow; the carpet soft and deeply piled. Pushing open a door on the first floor, she led me inside, and we stood in what I guessed must be the private sanctum of the late lamented wine importer. It was a pleasant enough room, though more of an office than a study as I had expected. Across one corner spread a vast desk, while behind it, inset in the wall, was a small safe, the door of which stood open.

Carol went straight to the desk and pointed to what lay on the polished surface. 'I found that lot in the safe,' she said. 'I don't pretend to understand them, but they certainly have some bearing on our difficulties. See what you can make of it all.'

The first thing I picked up was a short letter written in a long slanting hand on cheap notepaper. There was neither date-line, nor address, and the contents were brief. I read it aloud:

'Dear A. — If you can arrange to meet me or send a trusted agent to the address on the enclosed card, I think our business can be satisfactorily concluded. I now have everything ready, and am eager for you to keep your word and fulfil that promise you made. If you fail me, I do not answer for the consequences. — G.' I paused and glanced at my companion. 'That rather sounds as if they weren't quite such complete strangers as we were led to assume, doesn't it?'

She nodded thoughtfully.

'What else have we got?' I said. I picked up a small newspaper clipping and laid the letter aside. 'This looks interesting. Very interesting, in fact. You've read it, I suppose?'

'Yes, and I'm almost as much in the dark as ever.' Her eyes were troubled. If I had hoped to read anything in them, I failed.

The cutting was obviously several years old and taken from a French newspaper. I could find no indication of date or origin on it, and translated as I went: 'Among articles stolen from the residence of M. Paul Antoine, Parisian wine merchant, on Tuesday night was a valuable sapphire ring reputed to have been part of collection of the Emperor Napoleon III. The lock of the front door of Mr. Antoine's house had been forced, and the police are understood to have found important clues to the identity of the criminal. Mystery was added to the theft by the finding of a note addressed to M. Antoine in an unknown handwriting. Our special correspondent was fortunate enough to obtain the text of this cryptic message. 'One day, my friend,' it read, 'you will be glad I robbed you. The ring is my omen. From its possession, many things shall grow. — G.' An arrest is expected within the course of a few hours.'

I looked from the faded scrap of paper to meet the wide eyes of Carol Marney.

They were lovely eyes, but they didn't help me. 'Well,' I said grimly, 'does it make sense to you?'

She shook her head. 'Only to the extent of making everything more complicated than before.'

I sat down at the desk and tried to think things out, putting my deliberations into words as I did so. 'One thing is quite clear. Obviously Antoine *did* know Gaston. There was some connection between them in the past about which we know nothing. It's also plain that all this talk of Nazi wealth and Resistance work by the Frenchman is so much eyewash.'

'But is it?' she cut in. 'What about Gaston's warning to us last night? If he hadn't died, he would have told us all we wanted to know, and everything would have been plain sailing. You can look at it whichever way you like, but my idea is this: I'm more inclined than ever to believe Antoine's story to me as being true — in part, anyway. I admit that there must have been something between them in the past, probably something pretty shady. But according to my view, they had at last come to terms over some deal of which we are ignorant. If I'm not very much mistaken, the whole thing hinges on this sapphire ring that's mentioned in that newspaper cutting. Remember, Gaston also spoke of it — at a time, mark you, when he knew he was dying. It must be important, and it must be the same one. I'm certain it will prove to be the key to everything, if only we can find out how it fits.'

She stopped and looked me straight in the eyes. 'Then there's Christine,' she went on quietly. 'I'm a little uncertain of myself there, but I found something in the safe that I've not yet shown you.'

From behind her back she brought a photograph and handed it to me. It was little bigger than a snapshot, somewhat blurred and out of focus, but clear enough to recognise without difficulty.

'But . . . but it's a photo of you, Carol,' I said. 'Where's the mystery? I don't see any.'

'Look on the back.' Her eyes gleamed oddly as she spoke.

I turned the card over and found some

writing on the reverse side. Neatly printed in a small hand were the words: 'My beautiful godchild Christine. London, 1940.' And underneath: 'Rings on her fingers if G. has his way.'

'So *you're* Christine!' I gasped. 'Why on earth didn't you tell me before? Just what are you playing at?' I felt confused and exasperated; angry at being made a fool of, as I thought. I flung the photo on the desk and jumped to my feet, moving round it so that I faced her squarely.

'Come on,' I snapped. 'If you don't talk straight for once, I'm going to the police immediately.'

'Listen,' she said steadily, her gaze unwavering before my anger, 'I had no more idea that I was Christine than you did. I know it sounds insane, but it happens to be true. I've always been Carol Marney until this moment. That's my name, and it's the only one I've ever had as far as I know. What it all means I can't understand, but I want to clear it up as badly as you do.'

She paused for breath, staring at me appealingly to see what effect her outburst had had. For the life of me, I couldn't see a hand in front of my nose. The tangle in which I found myself grew thicker and thicker the further I went. Whatever happened, I was determined to unravel it; but how that was to be done I failed to comprehend. However, being angry with Carol was not one of the things that would help at all.

'Come downstairs and have some coffee with me,' I said in a quieter tone. 'We'll talk this thing over in a reasonable manner and try to make something intelligent out of it, if that's possible. Besides, you've had nothing to eat yet.' I grinned at her then; I couldn't help it. The look of tension in her face died away and she seemed to relax. I liked her a lot better that way. 'You've nothing more to show me while we're up here?'

'Nothing. Haven't you seen enough?'

'Not by half,' I answered as I led her through the door and down the stairs to the hall. 'But I think it'd be as well to sort out what we have before looking for anything else. Inexplicable problems seem to crop up by the handful in this business.

We'll take it in easy stages from now on.'

I spoke cheerfully enough, though my brain was in a whirl, and I felt like a swimmer caught up in a bed of strangling seaweed.

Down in the breakfast-room, I took it upon myself play host and pour her coffee. She sat opposite me from the window, and I had to admit she made a remarkably attractive picture. Even if I couldn't quite make up my mind as to the part she was playing in our troubles, there was no getting away from that one fundamental fact. It was the only thing about the whole affair that I liked.

'Now then,' I began when we were settled. 'First of all, whose writing is that on your photo?'

'Antoine's.' Her reply came without the slightest hesitation.

'So you're his godchild? That seems to be established. Did you know you were?'

She shook her head gravely.

'Have you ever seen that photo before? And if so, how and when was it taken?'

Again she was unable to answer. Deeply puzzled, I tried another tack.

'What about your own people? If old Antoine was your godfather, he must have known them pretty well.'

'Now look,' she said patiently, 'that photo is dated 1940, and the first time I ever set eyes on Antoine was when he picked me up after the air raid that killed my folks. As I've already told you, that happened in 1941. My father certainly never mentioned him before that, and as far as I was concerned, the man was a complete stranger. What's more, he was always remarkably good to me when I was left alone in the world, and went out of his way to see that I lived well from then on.'

'You certainly seem sure of all that, anyhow,' I admitted. 'Let's go back a bit. Antoine had in his possession at one time a ring that was reputedly once a part of an emperor's collection. He loses it as the result of a theft that was probably committed by our friend Gaston. That gentleman infers in a note to Antoine, which he leaves at the scene of the crime, that one day the wine merchant will be only too pleased that he was robbed.' I raised an eyebrow and squinted at the ceiling. 'You agree with my supposition so far, I take it?'

'It's quite logical reasoning,' she admitted, though not without a hint of doubt in her voice.

'Now,' I went on, 'we apparently get a gap of several years. Whether we shall ever fill it in, I don't know. But the next time either the ring or Gaston are mentioned is last night. And then — note this — the ring is no longer in Gaston's possession, but presumably forms a part of this fabulous hoard of illegal wealth we were on the trail of.'

I tapped the top of the table to emphasise my words, and she smiled at the engrossed way in which I was arguing — or guessing. I grinned back. I was enjoying myself, and all previous tiredness was gone. I felt fresh and fit and eager to get things straight. There must be some head and tail to the chaos. I found my brain functioning clearly, and quickly began to put forward a hypothetical case that had suggested itself during the last few moments of thought.

'Just suppose,' I said, 'that this ring was by way of being a lever through which Gaston hoped to gain something from Antoine. What it could have been, I have no idea.' I shrugged. 'I'm merely suggesting it as a possible solution. For instance, it might have been of such great value — either intrinsic or sentimental — to the wine merchant that he would have been prepared to bargain with Gaston for its return, or agree to his demands.'

I paused. Then: 'Judging from that letter, Gaston was looking forward to the conclusion of some deal, and my guess is that it was based on the ring. Before Gaston can take any steps, however, he loses his one lever in some way and is forced to fade out of the picture.'

I stopped and lit a cigarette, Carol waiting patiently for me to continue.

'I'm only guessing that part, of course,' I went on. 'I may be hopelessly wrong, but that's how it strikes me. So far so good. Now then. Antoine is the victim of a further burglary during the war here in England — you told me that bit yourself, remember? If the story about the Nazi cache is to be believed — and it's quite possible that it is true — his property becomes part of it; and this, I think, is where Gaston comes into his own again.

'All this time he's been trying to regain possession of his precious sapphire ring, and in the end discovers not only its whereabouts, but that more of Antoine's stuff is with it, all ready and handy for the Nazis to turn into cash to pay their agents. Why it was never used, I don't know, but apparently it wasn't. Anyhow, knowing what he does, Gaston is then in a position to bargain with Antoine again, and writes that letter to him. Probably everything would have gone well had it not been for the fact that there are others also interested in this cache, and that's where the snags arose. Gaston himself said something about a man named Coolis beating us to it, if you remember.'

She nodded.

'Well,' I went on, 'there you are! To my own satisfaction I've reconstructed part of the mystery, but we're still just as much in the fog as ever over the rest of it. Have you got anything to suggest?'

'I've been thinking and listening at the same time,' she said. 'As far as it goes, your theory is sound, but it leaves so much in the air that for practical purposes I can't see it being a lot of help. Don't you think we might find out something more concrete if we had a look at this place, Frigate's Hard? From what Gaston said, it sounds as if it's the centre of attraction, so to speak, and if we nosed around a bit we might bring something to light.'

I stood up and gazed out of the window at the garden.

'First *find* Frigate's Hard!' I said a little unkindly. 'Do you know where it is?'

'No, but I think I can find out.' She walked across to the telephone by the wall. 'I've a friend who works in a travel agency. If she can't find it for us, no one will.'

'Go ahead,' I said, glad of the prospect of action that would follow if she was successful.

I watched her back as she talked into the instrument. It was a nice-looking back, straight and well-shaped, with good legs beneath it. *Who are you?* I wondered. *You can't be two people. Christine Somebody, or Carol Marney?* Either name was pleasant. Of the two, I think I preferred Carol, though I couldn't for the life of me tell which was her real name. That she was honest, I no longer had any doubt; but that there was something very strange behind it all, I was just as certain.

A moment later she broke in on my thoughts. 'Frigate's Hard,' she announced triumphantly, 'is the name of a very small hamlet on the coast of Suffolk. It has a church, three cottages, a post office, and a pub. When do we start?'

Her eyes were shining with eagerness, and the feeling was catching.

'You win.' I smiled. 'We're on our way!'

5

The weather was glorious, the roads were good, and we were full of hope in our new bid to clear the air of mystery. With full tanks and long hours of daylight ahead, I took the road for Frigate's Hard, driving fast and turning things over in my mind as we went.

It must have been somewhere about mid-day when I suddenly had the one stunning thought that was to change the whole course of our reasoning, clearing away much of the opaque curtain that hung between ourselves and the solution of one at least of the major problems of the affair.

For several hours I had been puzzling my head about Carol and the indisputable evidence of her double identity. Quite suddenly it hit me as solidly as a ton of bricks that there was a way in winch that seemingly impossible fact could come about.

I slammed on the brakes and pulled up with a jerk, swinging round to face my passenger. 'Carol Marney,' I said, 'were you an adopted child?'

For an instant she gaped at me in amazement. Her hand stole up to cover her pretty red mouth, and I thought she was going to cry out loud. And then, by infinitely slow degrees, she relaxed. When at last she spoke, her voice was barely more than a whisper. 'How did you know?'

'I didn't. It just came to me out of the blue. It's the only way in which you could possibly be both Christine and Carol. Good heavens, don't you see that this makes all the difference? It's nothing to be ashamed of. Why didn't you tell me before?'

'Because I never knew for certain,' she said. 'My people never said it in as many words, but I sometimes used to wonder. They were both such different physical types to myself that it seemed odd at times that I was really their daughter. Now you've come along and crystallised my doubts into certainty. It's a bit of a shock.'

'Yes, I suppose it must be,' I said gently. 'Sorry if I sprung it on you suddenly. I'm afraid I rather thought you knew all the time, and I wondered why you'd kept it back.'

'But what difference does it make?' Her voice was troubled. I bit my lip at that, cursing myself for being so impetuous. The inference to be drawn was not a particularly pleasant one.

'I'm afraid it means that in your past life you must have been linked in some way with friend Gaston,' I said at last. 'Don't,' I hastened to add, 'think that that's necessarily a bad thing, but I must admit it brings you rather close to the heart of the business.' I paused for a moment. 'Carol, what exactly *do* you know about yourself?'

'Only what I've already told you. To the best of my knowledge I've always been Carol Marney, and I never remember anyone else but the people I looked on as my parents. I can't understand it, but it certainly looks as if you're likely to have hit the nail on the head. The idea of me being an adopted child makes things clearer, doesn't it?'

'Or thicker,' I replied grimly. I was wondering of Gaston lying there in York. What, if any, I wondered desperately, was the relationship between that mean-looking little Frenchman and this peerless woman at my side? None, I hoped, but I should feel better if I could be certain.

I set the car in motion again, and for a while we drove in silence. I was averse to put too many of my thoughts into words, and she, I think, was still a little stunned by our latest revelation. At length, however, she did what I had not the nerve to do. She spoke the very words that had nagged at my mind ever since the idea of her being Christine Somebody had entered my head.

'Do you . . . do you think that the man in York could have been my real father?' she asked very quietly.

I stole a sidewise glance at her face. Obviously she liked the idea about as much as I did.

'Well,' I replied carefully, 'I don't want to speak ill of the dead, but quite frankly he didn't strike me as the sort of father

I'd want. You wouldn't want him to be yours, I take it?'

'No. No, I . . . I don't think I should.' Her lower lip quivered. I thought she was going to burst into tears at first, but somehow she managed to hold them back. 'What am I going to do?' she asked tremulously.

I wished I could tell her. At that moment I'd have given anything to have been able to tell her all she wanted to know, but the fact was that I knew no more than she did.

'I shouldn't worry,' I said quietly. 'Whatever Gaston might have been in your early life, he's dead now, and he's left us with the most unholy mess to sort out. We'll bring it all down to basic facts in time, I've no doubt. But for the moment, I admit it's all a bit complicated. We've got to tread softly or we'll slip right over the edge into the deepest part and never get out again.'

'All right,' she said. 'I won't worry about it anymore — at least, I'll try not to. I just hope it all works out in the end, though.'

'So do I. As far as hard facts go, we have quite a few. The latest addition being the knowledge that for some reason into which we need not probe just now, the man Gaston had a definite intention of presenting you with a certain ring. First of all he stole it from Antoine, then lost it himself, and later ran it to earth again among a lot of Nazi riches, hidden, presumably, in the vicinity of Frigate's Hard. For the moment I think we should do well to concentrate on one thing at a time. Don't you agree?'

She nodded, suggesting a few seconds later that we should stop somewhere for a drink before completing the journey.

'Excellent,' I said happily, and a mile or two further on we pulled up at a wayside inn.

The beer was good and the landlord cheerful, so that presently we felt better both in body and soul. No longer did the clouds of mystery seem to hang so heavily around us, and I turned my thoughts for the first time since meeting Carol to what the future might hold for myself. The position I had been on my way to take up in Newcastle the previous night was a sound one; and though I had said I should probably turn up that day, I knew I had plenty of time to play with, since my arrangements had only been of a tentative nature. In actual fact, it would make little difference if I failed to present myself until the following week, and in view of the circumstances I realised how lucky I was to be so placed.

'How much further have we got to go?' asked my companion, breaking in on my train of thought.

'Not more than about twenty miles. We ought to be there in half an hour at the most. I've a hunch that things are going to be quite interesting when we've got our bearings. I also think I shall like the place. D'you know Suffolk at all?'

'No. I've never been there myself, but Antoine once spent a weekend with some friends somewhere near Ipswich. He was full of it when he came back.'

'That reminds me,' I said. 'I think we ought to check up and make absolutely sure he was the laddie that was killed in the Mercedes. Hang on here while I ring up the Grantham police. I won't be very long.'

'Aren't they likely to be a little suspicious if you start asking questions about the accident?'

'I don't see why they should be. But I tell you what — why don't you ring them? You've a much better excuse than I have, and they can't complain if you ask questions. After all, the man was your employer, and you've every right to know how it happened.'

'Yes,' she said. 'I'll do it.'

'Mind if I come and listen to the conversation?'

'Not a bit. Come on.'

In a few minutes we were through, and Carol was talking to the distant police station. Yes, the sympathetic sergeant at the other end was telling her, Mr. Antoine *had* been killed in a Mercedes. It had been a very bad accident, but she could be quite certain in her mind that the poor gentleman died instantly. He could have felt no pain. There was no shadow of doubt about it. He had a broken neck. That in itself would have been enough to kill him outright, and as well as that, there were other injuries. Both legs, for instance, were shattered below the knee, and the steering column had penetrated his chest. I watched her face intently as the words drifted thinly to my ears. She grew pale and her hand shook a little as it held the receiver. At the last grim details she swayed and closed her eyes. I put out an arm to support her, fearing she would fall.

'Poor kid,' I muttered half to myself. 'Whatever he was, you must have been fond of him, I suppose.'

A moment later she rang off with a barely audible word of thanks and stood looking at me.

'Chin up,' I said gently. 'Let's have another drink. You look as if you need one badly. I'm sorry you had to hear all the gruesome details. If I'd known he was going to tell you all that, I'd never have suggested you speaking.'

'I'm all right,' she whispered. 'Leave me alone and let me think. I'm all tangled up at the moment. Both legs, he said, didn't he?'

I nodded. 'It must have been an awful mess.'

'But you don't understand. It couldn't have been!'

'What on earth do you mean?'

Her eyes were cool and clear and steady as she regarded me. The faintest smile touched her lips for an instant and then was gone again.

'Paul Antoine had one artificial leg,' she said quietly. 'The man in the Mercedes simply couldn't have been him. That's all.'

6

Without a word, I led her back to the bar. Things that before had appeared clear became clouded; one part of my brain felt elated at the news she had given me, while another shouted aloud that the thing was growing to be a nightmare, twisting and turning like a snake in the darkness.

I leaned against the polished oak of the counter. For some reason I felt like leaning on something solid. Carol sank into a chair close by, watching my face as if hoping to find in it a lead to guide her through the thicket of our problems.

With more beer in my hand, I felt equal to the task of thinking and talking again. We were alone in the place, so it suited my purpose well, for it stood in an isolated position on the edge of a lonely tract of common land.

'You're quite positive of this?' I said at length.

'Absolutely. He lost a leg below the knee in the 1914 war at Cambrai. He was very sensitive about it and got quite angry once when I suggested that it would save him a lot of trouble if he had his rooms all on the ground floor. He said that if other people could climb stairs he was sure he could, and even went so far as to tell me to mind my own business.'

'I see,' I said reflectively. 'Then we're more or less back where we started, aren't we? I mean, if we are to presume that Antoine isn't dead, it opens up all sorts of fresh channels. Not only that, but it also puts the man in a slightly more favourable light as far as I'm concerned. Looked at from this new angle, it boils down to the fact that he seems to have been a victim of foul play as much as we were. Unless, of course, he wanted to disappear, and took the opportunity of effecting a quick change-over of identity with the second man in the Mercedes when it crashed.'

'But why should he want to disappear?'

'I'm sure I don't know. There's a whole lot I don't know, and that's only one of many things. Let's be charitable and assume that he didn't want to disappear. Where does it lead us? And what can we draw from it?'

'There's only one answer to that; he must have been kidnapped by the same men who killed Gaston. I'd stake everything I've got on the belief that Antoine would do nothing to harm me. I just can't believe he was the man who tried to wreck us on the road last night. It doesn't make sense with what I know of his nature.'

I grunted a reluctant agreement. 'Then he's either dead or held captive somewhere. There's no other solution. He must have come into contact with the man called Coolis sometime last night, because his identity papers were apparently found on the body in the car. My idea is that he received a phone message from them — probably couched in terms that would bring him running — and that he walked straight into a trap. The times we have would make it quite feasible. Bulmers told us he had a phone call about seven and went out shortly afterwards. Suppose he was picked up almost immediately by the Mercedes? They could have been in York by the time we got there. They'd have to motor pretty fast, I know, but in a car like that it certainly wouldn't have been impossible.'

'Then you mean that when my handbag was stolen it was Coolis that did it, and that Antoine was outside in the car all the time?'

'Whether it was Coolis who actually took it, I don't know. Remember there must have been two crooks in that car. You can't drive and shoot out of the passenger side at the same time, and that's what happened. I wish I'd known that Mercedes was near the inn when I was idling at the bar! I might have done something about it then.'

'It's a wonder we didn't hear it,' she replied with a smile. 'It made enough noise when it overtook us on the road, didn't it?'

I stiffened at the words, then smacked a hand to my forehead as a new thought flashed through my mind. 'Holy smoke!' I gasped. 'You've made it worse instead of better. Listen — I wasn't more than half a minute behind Coolis after he took your bag. When I reached the yard he was gone, but I could hear the car accelerating away down the road. It was going fast, and there was no other motor within earshot. But the car I heard was definitely not a Mercedes.'

She furrowed her brow at that, trying to find out what I was getting at and where it led us. 'Then there must have been two cars,' she said. 'They must have used another one at the Tawny Owl, and kept the Mercedes for the fast run to York. I don't see what you're getting so excited about.'

'Because,' I answered eagerly, 'it sets me thinking on a different line. What's been puzzling me up to now has been why these men took the trouble to steal that card from your handbag if they already had Antoine with them. Gaston would have given up the secret without question when he saw him. They didn't even have to have the card for the address — they could have got that out of Antoine with a little persuasion, because he knew where you were supposed to meet the

Frenchman.' I paused. 'Don't you see what I'm getting at?'

She shook her head in bewilderment. 'Frankly, I don't.'

'This is what I think — I believe we're up against two different parties, both after the same thing. It makes sense, doesn't it?'

'It may do to you, but I can't see it yet.'

'Well, if we work on this new theory of mine, a lot of things become easier to understand. This is what I think happened. Antoine hears from Gaston. Two other interested parties also get wind of his discovery of the cache. Both connect it in some way with the wine merchant — how, I don't know. That doesn't matter for the moment. And both take steps to gain the secret, or stop Antoine getting it from Gaston. Clear so far?'

She nodded. 'Yes. Go on.'

'One party seizes Antoine himself and extracts the York address, taking him with them. The other works on you and gets its information from your handbag. How they knew it was there I can't imagine, but I'm guessing a lot of this, so it's bound to be sketchy. The attack on us was made to prevent our reaching York; and seeing that it came from the Mercedes, it means that both parties must know you by sight.'

I paused and looked at her. 'When I first saw you in the Tawny Owl,' I went on, 'I had an idea that you were a little frightened when that man came in and walked towards you. Had you ever seen him before?'

'Not to my knowledge. But I did have a feeling that his face was slightly familiar in some way. I didn't like the look of him, and I suppose I must have shown it in my expression. That's probably what gave you the idea.'

'Maybe. Anyhow, the point is that if I'm right, one crowd reached York and found Gaston, and I think they were the ones that had your card, because he never mentioned Antoine at all, if you remember. It follows then that Coolis was the man who took your bag, going straight on to York and accrediting himself with that card you had. The other party came along later, found they were too late, and made a dash for Frigate's Hard on the heels of Coolis. How does that sound?'

'How would they know where to go?'

I scratched my head, finding myself becoming as much entangled as I had ever been. Somehow now that I had put my thoughts into words like this, they didn't sound nearly so convincing; and yet I felt certain that somewhere in the idea I had put forward there must be some grain of truth.

'I don't know,' I said at last. 'The only thing I can think is that they got that much out of Gaston before leaving. I've got myself all tied up again. I suggest we give things a chance to sort themselves out, and have a look at this famous Frigate's Hard before anything else happens to stop us.' I glanced at my watch. 'Do you realise we've been sitting here for nearly an hour and a half nattering away and getting nowhere?'

'I wouldn't say we'd got nowhere,' she replied. 'After all, we do know that Antoine may not be dead.'

'*May not be* is right,' I said grimly. 'Come on, let's move.'

7

The remainder of the journey to Frigate's Hard was uneventful, but my first impression of the place itself stands out in my memory to this day.

With the sun behind us, we ran down a long sloping road that was little better than a lane, then dipped sharply to bring the village into view. You couldn't call it beautiful by any stretch of imagination. Rather, it possessed a sort of melancholy attraction. Behind the small cluster of cottages stood the tall-steepled church, far too big for the size of the place, and evidence of the days when the population must have been many times greater.

I'd seen the same kind of thing in East Anglia before — a large and imposing church with hardly a house in sight. Probably, I reflected, Frigate's Hard had once been quite a prosperous little fishing port; and then, I imagined, the river on which it stood had become silted up and useless, hence the decay and almost entire disappearance of the village.

Whatever its past history might have been, however, I found the hamlet attractive in its own somewhat strange and forlorn way. In the distance, possibly a mile away, the sea sparkled and danced brilliantly; but close in, no more than a few yards from the buildings themselves, I saw the low-lying mud flats stretching out on either side of a sluggish stream of water.

Not far from where the road entered the place, the inlet petered out altogether; and if there had ever been a river of any magnitude, it must have long since dried up and vanished. Vivid green water meadows spread serenely away into the haze to north and south, while perhaps two miles from where we stood rose the grim, hard outline of an old Martello tower, worthless legacy of the days when Napoleon tried to create a precedent that Hitler sought to emulate.

The very thought and sight of the ancient relic brought me back to remembrance of Carol and the ring that seemed in some inexplicable way to be linked with her past history. Try as I would, I could see nothing but the mist of intrigue that swirled about our minds.

There was an air of drowsy somnolence about the whole place that was catching, and I could quite easily have pulled up then and there and gone to sleep. Thinking it over afterwards, it was hardly surprising, seeing that neither of us had had any sleep the previous night.

Pausing at a spot on the slope above the village from where we could get a comprehensive view of its layout, we scanned as much as we could see for any indication that there were other visitors besides ourselves.

'That looks as if it might be the pub,' I said, pointing to a white low-roofed building that stood facing the shallow water of the only portion of the inlet that was clear of mud. Plastered across the wall that presented itself to our eyes was a large advertisement for cider, though I could not see the traditional inn sign swinging in the breeze at the front of the house.

Ranged on either side of this were several other small cottages fronting a patch of refreshingly green grass, while the church stood aloof some hundreds of yards back. Beyond it was a building that I decided must be the vicarage, a rambling place of beam and stone that must have been a strain on the pocket of any incumbent. What small part we could see of the grounds was, in fact, nothing more than an unkempt tangle of under-growth and weeds.

'Let's go down and have a look round,' said Carol beside me. 'I can't see any sign of a car, or life at all for that matter, can you?'

'No,' I said. 'It certainly looks sleepy enough. Hardly what you'd call a hive of industry, is it?'

I let in the clutch and motored down the hill, keeping my eyes open all the time, for I felt it would be a shame to run into Coolis or anyone else connected with our affair before we had time to see how the land lay and what was happening in this drowsy corner of England.

My companion's first description of the

place as being composed of little more than three cottages was an exaggeration — there were at least nine or ten, one of which I identified as the post office-cum-general shop. The main street, down which we made our way, was wide and dusty, running straight to a small wooden jetty, where it ended abruptly with the muddy water lapping in gentle wavelets round the slimy piles.

Outside the inn hung a notice informing anyone interested that teas could be obtained on the premises. Thinking it would be a way of getting to know something more about the place, we stopped and walked through the gate that led to the garden at the rear.

We were greeted by a plump cheerful-faced woman who took our order with a pleasant smile, then bustled away, leaving us to make ourselves comfortable at a small round table beneath a bower of rustic wood. For a moment I leaned back contentedly and gazed about. The setting was attractive, and I felt well pleased with life in spite of the tortuous mystery that beset us on every side. Possibly Carol had something to do with that, for she was good company, seeming to fit in with my every mood from the moment I first laid eyes on her.

'Well,' she said, leaning forward a little towards me, 'we're here. But what happens next? We can hardly ask the local inhabitants if they've seen any suspicious characters, can we? What do you suggest we do?'

'It's five o'clock now,' I answered. 'The bar will be open in an hour, and that's usually the accepted place to gather information. We'll try our luck there. Leave it to me.'

But the bar was not to be the place from which we were to glean our knowledge. Our hostess returned as I finished speaking and placed a well-laden tray on the table before us.

'There you are, sir. I think you'll find those scones very tasty. The gentleman who was here earlier said they were the nicest he'd ever had.'

'I suppose you have quite a few visitors?' I said.

'Well, sir, we used to have, but not so

many nowadays. People can't afford the petrol to come this far, you see. You're only the second party we've had all week, apart from the gentleman this afternoon. He told me he'd come from London to do some sketching.' She sniffed disdainfully. 'Can't see what he'd find round here to draw, but you never know with these artists.'

'That's a fact,' I replied. To hear that someone else was in the village interested me. 'He'll be staying here with you, I suppose?' I asked casually.

'No, sir. Got one of them caravan things behind a motorcar. Nice-looking outfit, but I'd rather have a proper roof over me head if you ask me. Got it up near the rectory. They tell me he pulled in just about midday.'

'Well, I hope he finds plenty to sketch,' I said with a laugh.

'I expect he will at that, sir. Anyhow, it's all extra custom for us, and we can do with it. There now, though, I'm keeping you from your tea; it'll all be cold. Just give a call at the door when you've finished, sir.'

Carol was already pouring out as she bustled away, and her eyes twinkled as she caught my glance.

'It's all right for you to laugh,' I said with a grin, 'but I'm going to have a look at this artist. It's just possible that he's the one who tried to paint us out with a gun last night.'

From tea we progressed to beer. The interior of the bar was a cosy enough picture, with its great open fireplace and old oak settles; and for a while we sat there alone, till presently a few customers began to drift in through the door. I was thinking about the man who had arrived from London that morning, and wondering if he could be any connection with the mystery, when something happened that put all thought of it from my head.

We were settling down to our second glass, and keeping our ears open for gossip of any kind that might prove useful, when the door opened and a tall well-dressed man entered the place. He gave a cheerful 'Good evening' to the landlord and ordered a whisky; then, leaning back against the bar and glancing round the room with lively eyes, he caught sight of Carol at my side. What gave me the impression that he recognised her immediately I am uncertain, but it was very definite, and I felt myself stiffen tensely. He made no sign, however, but sipped his drink and walked over to the fireplace, standing with his back to it and surveying the customers with a faintly amused expression on his face.

In spite of his apparent affability, I could not help disliking the fellow on sight. There was something too catlike about the way he moved, and his light grey eyes were never still for a second.

I would have said something to my companion about him had we not been within a couple of yards of where he stood, and I did not want to draw attention to the fact that I had noticed him too openly. Instead I gave her a gentle nudge, but already her eyes were taking in all there was to be seen.

And then, as sometimes happens in a fairly crowded room, there was a sudden lull in conversation during which a sound came clearly to my ears. It was a sound that made my pulse race madly. The stranger by the fireplace was humming a tune, and the tune was that of 'Lili Marlene.'

8

Instantly my mind skated back to the sordid little hovel in York and the slurring words of the dying man on the floor: 'Whatever you do, be careful of Lili Marlene.'

Was it just one of those queer coincidences? I wondered. Or had we run up against the very person he had warned us about? I couldn't be sure, and yet I hadn't taken to the man by the fireplace from the first. I'd never seen him before, and neither did I think Carol had; but there war that one fleeting impression that he had recognised her.

We had been warned to beware of a name, or a song, or a tune; I didn't really know which had been meant. It was all so conjectural that I felt hopelessly uncertain of myself. But as far-fetched as it was, there was no getting away from the fact that here at Frigate's Hard, which I regarded as the heart of the affair, was something happening that I could not afford to overlook. I had to find out more about the tall stranger who hummed so unconcernedly to himself as he surveyed the gathering of locals and sipped his drink with an air of well-being that was somehow disturbing.

'Let's take a walk in the fresh air,' I said to Carol. 'We can come back for another drink later on.'

She knew what I meant all right, and a moment later we were standing in the golden sunlight of early evening. We stood side by side leaning over the rickety rail that formed the only protection between the end of the road and the water of the inlet.

'I don't like it,' I said quietly. 'It's too good to be true, but I've a horrid feeling that that man isn't all he seems the surface. What did Gaston mean by that remark about Lili Marlene? There must be some connection.'

'It's certainly fishy,' she admitted. 'What about this artist the old lady mentioned? D'you think it might be a good idea to have a look at him as well while we're about it? If the man in the bar is phony, and your suspicions about the artist have any foundation, there might be some link between them.'

The suggestion revived my interest in what we had heard earlier. 'Wouldn't do any harm,' I agreed. 'Come on.'

We turned and strolled back through the village and bore up towards the rectory.

'Will the car be all right?' she wanted to know. I'd left it in a small yard behind the inn. There wasn't a proper car park, and as far as I could see it was the only car in the whole place. Certainly I hadn't laid eyes on another since our arrival.

'Yes,' I said. 'They don't steal cars in this sort of city.'

A winding path overgrown here and there with briars and low hanging bushes took us in the general direction of the house. I saw the tyre marks of a fairly large car in softer patches of the track surface, and guessed they must be those of the car that had drawn the artist's caravan.

By following them, we soon found

ourselves working towards a broad meadow that lay beyond the rectory. Pausing at the gate that opened into this, I leaned over and tried to get a sight of the van itself. Faint tyre marks again pointed the way for my eyes; and there at the far end of the field, drawn up in the shadow of a high hedge, was the object of our search.

The caravan itself was a luxurious-looking affair, painted cream, and must have been a four-berth model. Some yards distant stood the towing car, a big Lanchester saloon that looked as if it had seen several years' service. Signs of life there were none, and I wondered where the occupant might be.

'If we go up the line of hedge,' suggested Carol, 'we can reach a spot right behind it and have a closer look without being seen ourselves.'

'Good idea,' I replied, and off we set. We trod with care, for I had no mind to advertise our curiosity if it could be avoided; and how glad we were to be for our caution was proved by subsequent events.

Arriving at the corner of the hedge, we turned through a right angle and headed for where the van stood. The hedge was thick, and only a sudden flash of cream showing through the dark leaves told us when we were level with it. I put a finger to my lips for silence, for I thought I caught the faint sound of voices. Of this I could not be sure, but was taking no chances. If there was anything to be gained by eavesdropping I was perfectly prepared to listen with a clear conscience.

We covered the last few yards on hands and knees, then put our heads close together in a small gap among the roots of the tangle of bushes that formed the hedge. From this point I could only see about three square feet of the van, but I had been right about the voices, though what was actually being said I was unable to hear. Quite suddenly they stopped, and then the strains of music took their place.

'Wireless!' I breathed disgustedly.

'It shows someone's at home, anyway,' she whispered.

I nodded at that. 'Yes,' I said. 'You're right there. Let's see if he shows himself.'

I think we were both totally unprepared for what happened next. We must have lain where we were for fully ten minutes without any sign of our vigil being rewarded, when I heard the sound of footfalls on the grass of the meadow beyond the hedge. Somebody was walking in the direction of the van; walking fast and with a definite purpose in his stride.

I strained my neck in an effort to see through the gap before my eyes, but could see nothing until the footsteps were almost on top of us. Then they halted and I heard a man's voice call out sharply. The lower part of two legs came into my range of vision, and I found myself looking at the brown tan shoes that I had so recently noticed on the feet of the humming customer in the inn — Lili Marlene I christened him, for want of a better name.

The sight of his feet sent my nerves tingling with a rare feeling of anticipation. There came the sound of a door being opened and a second pair of feet appeared before my nose. I pressed

Carol's hand for absolute silence and together we listened as if our very lives depended on it.

Without being able to see the faces of the two men, I was able to pick out the voice of the man from the inn, since I'd heard him order his drink. The other person spoke in a deep, rather rumbling kind of accent. Hardly daring to breathe, we listened.

'So you got here all right, Henry?' It was the artist speaking.

'More by luck than judgment, my friend,' replied the other man. 'I'm lucky to be alive, actually. We had a smash on the way down last night. Coolis was killed, and I only escaped by the skin of my teeth.'

'What about A.? You had him with you, didn't you?'

'He's safe enough. Badly shaken, but I managed to keep him quiet till all the fuss was over. He's officially dead, only he doesn't know it yet! I had to keep him under cover till the breakdown gang finished clearing up the mess. Then we came on here.'

'Where have you got him now?'

'Never you mind that. I tell you he's safe enough. I fixed him up on the way — you don't think I brought him right to the door, do you?' The question was derisive.

'All right, all right. I only asked, didn't I? Any other hitches?'

'None. I got the details from York before Gaston realised the old man wasn't there of his own free will. You should have seen his face when he found out he'd been tricked! He tried to get nasty, of course, but Coolis knocked him out for the count and we left as fast as we could.'

'So Coolis is dead?' The words were quiet and, reflective, as if the speaker was trying to decide what would come as a result.

'Dead as mutton, my friend. That only leaves you and I.'

'Have you forgotten Rathmore? He's dangerous.'

'Maybe he would be if he was here, but unless he happens to be psychic, I can't see how he can guess where we are, or where the stuff is. I'm certain he never got a smell of us after we left London with A. From then on we moved fast, and if it hadn't been for Coolis driving like a madman I'd have been here hours ago.'

'I hope you're right, Henry. Frankly I'm a little nervous. In fact, I'll be damned glad when we get away from here. When shall we pick the stuff up?'

'Tonight, of course! There's no sense in wasting more time than we have to. We'd better not be seen together. I'll meet you at the crossroads outside the village at eleven.'

'Suits me. What are you going to do now?'

'Perigrin should be here with the boat soon. I'd best go and meet him. There's an anchorage not far from the place that will come in very handy.'

'You're being very close about this hiding place. Can you tell me where it is?'

'No. The less you know, the less you can tell if anything does happen to go wrong. I'll see you right, don't worry.'

'There's nothing else for me to do, is there?'

'No.' The retort was sharp, almost

menacing. I heard the man from the inn shift his feet as if to move off, and then he hesitated. 'By the way,' he said in a slightly less truculent tone, 'have you seen anything of a young couple knocking round here today? They were in the pub when I arrived, and I'm sure I've seen the woman somewhere before.'

'No one's been round here since I pulled in this morning.'

'Hmm. Must be imagining things, I suppose.'

'Who do you think it might be? You make me jumpy with all this talk of strangers. Forget it, for heaven's sake, and let's get out of here as soon as we can.'

Lili Marlene, however, was persistent. I could tell he was still suspiciously turning the idea over in his mind. 'Have you seen a car of any sort today?'

There was a slight pause during which I suppose the bogus artist was trying to remember. At length: 'Yes, I did see a big sports motor come down the hill this afternoon, but I've not seen anything of it since. Why?'

'I'm probably barking up the wrong

tree, but I'd like to get a sight of that car. You don't know it, my friend, but it was a big sports car that Coolis saw the woman in last night. I was driving at the time, so I never got a glimpse of her face, but he said it was her all right — old A.'s secretary, I mean — and he took a shot at the driver. I think they crashed, but we didn't stop to see. The road was too dark to see either of them at all clearly, but as I say there was something sort of familiar about that wench I saw in the pub down the lane. Wish I could have been sure. I'd know the car anywhere, though — a scarlet Bentley, one of the old ones.'

'Hell! That's what the one I saw today was!'

For a moment there was a dead silence, then I heard Lili Marlene move off. 'I'll see you later,' he called over his shoulder. 'And whatever you do, keep your mouth shut. I've got some work to do!'

With that he was gone, and I could hear his hurrying footsteps fading in the distance. I was left with an uncomfortable feeling that the work he mentioned had to do with our possible extermination. I glanced at Carol. Her face was white and set, and I knew she had drawn as much from the conversation as I had. While it cleared the air of much of the riddle that had gone before, it presented as well a heap of new difficulties.

One thing was painfully obvious: the man from the inn would not take kindly to our presence in the district. He had clearly been in the Mercedes at the time of the attack on us, and if he found us again, I had no doubt at all in my mind that he would show no hesitation in making a second bid to eliminate us from the scene of action. Lili Marlene, in fact, was a man to be treated with respect, like a dangerous snake.

By the time Lili Marlene was out of earshot, the so-called artist had withdrawn into the interior of his temporary home, and I decided it was a suitable moment to fade away ourselves. By a slight pressure on Carol's fingers, I attracted her attention and put my lips against her small shell-like ear. 'Let's go somewhere we can talk,' I muttered.

Wriggling cautiously away, we presently

got to our feet and walked down the hedge again the way we had come.

'Well,' I said, 'what do you make of it now?'

'I'm not sure,' she said. 'One thing is clear: Antoine is alive, though where he is we don't know, and as far as I can see it wouldn't be too healthy to show our faces in the village again.'

'You're right there,' I said grimly. 'That means the car's in baulk and we can't touch it till we know what's happening.'

'And at eleven o'clock tonight they propose to collect this cache of stuff and disappear. What'll happen to Antoine after that, I wonder?' She sounded worried. So was I. 'They'll hardly let him go free, will they?'

'Not likely. More probably they'll kill Mm quietly and leave no trace behind them.'

I felt that now as never before I had to think clearly and get things straight. Had I had a gun I might have attempted to find Lili Marlene and waylay him to get the information we needed, but I was not armed. For a while I toyed with the idea of walking into the caravan and trying to make the artist talk, but decided against that for the simple reason that he obviously knew very little himself. It would serve our purpose better, I realised, to make use of him as a means of finding out the layout for ourselves.

'If we lie low till later,' I said, 'and then keep the same appointment as he's going to, he'll be bound to lead us to what we want, namely the cache. What we can do when we get there I don't quite know, but it'll be something at any rate, and possibly we'll be able to take steps to rescue Antoine as well.'

'How about this boat that Lili spoke of?' said Carol. 'That might give us a line to follow in the meantime. I think they're meaning to use it to clear off in when the job's done.'

'The problem is to see without being seen,' I pointed out. 'Still, as you say, it's worth a look. If we get onto some high ground, we might get a sight of it. He said it was expected soon, and if that's the case we ought to see something before it actually arrives.'

We made our way to the crest of a low hillock that dominated the village, lying down on the grass in the last of the sunlight. From this vantage point, the country stretched all around except to our immediate front, where the sea was already beginning to grey over with the far-flung shadows of the coast.

For a while nothing rewarded us, but at last Carol touched my arm and pointed towards the south. Following her gaze, I made out the small shape of a motorboat creeping up the coast. As it gradually drew closer, we saw that it was in fact a fair-sized cruiser such as you see by the dozen in the Thames estuary, and which are capable of quite long voyages if their owners are not averse to cramped quarters.

At that moment I would have given a lot for a pair of binoculars, but not having any was compelled to make the best of it, keeping my eyes fixed on the growing shape of the vessel till it slowed and turned hesitantly into the shallow arm of sea that led to Frigate's Hard.

I think now that Lili Marlene must

have signalled it from the shore before ever it reached the village; for, shortly after turning in, it hove to and lay still on the muddy water. By straining our eyes till they ached, we could just make out the figure of a man in the well, and once I thought I saw his hand raised as if replying to someone invisible on the beach. Not long after that, he scrambled into the dinghy that towed astern and sculled himself ashore, disappearing from view round the shoulder of a small promontory.

Not many minutes later it reappeared, and this time there were two men in it, one of whom I guessed was undoubtedly our friend from the inn, Lili.

The opportunity was too good to be missed. He was clearly on his way to guide the cruiser round to wherever it was intended to lie, and in the meantime there was no reason why we should not regain the Bentley and at the same time reconnoitre the rendezvous that had been planned for eleven o'clock that night.

'Come on,' I said to Carol. 'This is where we do the big 'fade-out' act.'

Gripping her hand, I began to run down the hill towards the village. We arrived at the inn somewhat out of breath but otherwise without incident. The first thing I did was to make sure the car was where I had left it. At the time I ran it into the yard at the rear of the place, I had not thought of concealing it, but now I was glad its resting place had been out of sight.

Once satisfied that it was all right, we went into the bar for a final drink, making it clear to the landlord that we were returning to London and would have to be on our way at once. Having given him the impression that we were leaving Frigate's Hard for good, I turned the car and put it at the road that led up the hill and into the open country beyond. I hoped the bogus artist would hear and note our departure, for if he did it would bolster up the idea I had been careful to leave in the minds of the landlord of the inn and everyone else who had cared to listen. If my plan succeeded, even Lili Marlene might believe that we had gone; and unless he had actually seen the car, which I doubted, he might possibly accept our presence as a coincidence. Admittedly I was not particularly sanguine about that, for he struck me as the type of man who would harbour doubts in his mind until he had positive proof that they were nonexistent. However, there was nothing else I could do, and it now rested with Fate as to what would happen.

We had no difficulty in locating the crossroads that had been mentioned, and were lucky in another respect, too. Some yards down the lane that ran east was a shallow depression that looked as if it was probably all that was left of the efforts of some earlier generation to dig clay or something of the sort. Anyhow, whatever it might have been in the past, it now made an ideal hiding place for the Bentley, and without hesitation I motored right into it and we climbed out.

From the back of the car I took the metal jack handle, weighing it in my hands. Being unarmed as I was, it seemed only sensible to provide myself with a weapon of some kind. By that time it was growing dark, long shadows gathering round us. I was thankful for that, since it gave us additional cover and ensured that we were unlikely to be spotted from the crossroads.

The rendezvous lay a little below the level of our place of concealment, but by scaling a low bank and making our way to a further hedge, we were able to overlook the intersection without having to show ourselves at all. It was eight-thirty by the time we settled down to wait, and I realised then that we could have made use of the hours before us more profitably had we tried to find out where the cruiser was anchored. However, it was too late now to think of that, and anyway rapidly growing too dark to see very far. The air had a smell of rain in it, and I hoped we were not in for a wetting, though at the moment the weather certainly seemed to promise fair enough for our wants.

All manner of thoughts and questions ran through my brain as we waited there on the lonely edge of the bank with our eyes fixed on the narrow crossing of the two dusty roads. I wondered how Lili

Marlene had reached Frigate's Hard; whether he had a car hidden somewhere; where he was holding Antoine; and finally what kind of desperate danger we were likely to meet that night.

For the hundredth time, I wished I was armed. Though things were clearer in my understanding now, I knew well enough that we were up against as dangerous a gang of men as I could well imagine.

Some of the time we talked in whispers, sorting out the sequence of events into a fairly tangible whole. It was Carol who set the ball rolling by asking me if I had any idea who the man Rathmore was. I remembered the artist mentioning the name as if he was a potential enemy to them.

'There's only one person he can be as far as I can see,' I answered, 'and that's the man who stole your bag at the Tawny Owl. Obviously from what we now know, it wasn't Coolis who took it, since he had Antoine with him and there was therefore no need for him to have the card of introduction. Besides, Lili never said anything about that episode, and he certainly would have done so had they had a hand in it. Who or what Rathmore is I've no idea, but I'd recognise him again without any trouble, wouldn't you? For one thing, he limped badly when he was in the pub. I remember how surprised I was at the speed with which he moved in spite of it.'

She nodded. 'Yes, I noticed that, too. I wish I could understand all this. I suppose Rathmore is part of the other crowd that's after the cache?'

'Must be,' I said. 'Lili and Co. don't know it, but after getting what he wanted from your bag he did follow on to York, and what's more he got there before we did. The trouble was that he reached Gaston too late. Why, I don't know, but it must have been him who killed the Frenchman. It wasn't Coolis, because you noticed that Lili said he merely knocked him out before they left. My guess is that Rathmore was so furious at being beaten to it that he killed the man out of sheer spite. Whether he got any information out of him first, I don't know, but whatever happened this crowd think they've lost him. Personally I rather hope they have, because things are complicated enough as it is without having anybody else on the scene.'

'What I can't understand is how Coolis knew I was in the Bentley with you when we were attacked.'

I shrugged. 'All I can suggest is that either Coolis knew you well enough by sight to recognise you as they went past, or more probably, perhaps, they had someone tailing you from the time you left London. Rathmore, of course, must have done something like that, and it's quite on the cards that the others have been watching you as well.'

'I wish I knew where I come into the picture myself,' she said. 'Why on earth should Gaston want me to have a ring I've never heard of? And how do I happen to be Antoine's godchild?'

I frowned. I didn't want her to worry herself about things like that, as we had no means of discovering. 'Maybe if we're lucky enough to find any trace of Antoine, he'll be able to tell us all that — and the rest.'

'There's nothing else we can do, is there?'

'No. We can only wait and contain ourselves as patiently as possible.'

I glanced at my watch as I finished speaking. It was barely ten o'clock, but it was at that moment that we both heard the first faint sound of footsteps on the surface of the road that came from our right, and would take the traveller down to the village. Tensely we waited and listened, wondering if this was simply some harmless local inhabitant making his way home, or a person who might have some far more sinister part in the mystery in which we moved so blindly.

In the darkness I met Carol's eyes. She smiled a little and I answered her, taking her fingers in my own as the footsteps drew nearer. In the distance a train whistled; from somewhere a long way off came the mournful hoot of an owl. I caught the sound of a cough not twenty yards from where we lay. It began to rain slightly. The noise of approach grew louder; and with a sudden dawning of dread at the back of my mind, I realised that the man on the road was scuffling the dirt at every step he took.

Uneven and muffled though the sound was, I knew then that he walked with a limp.

9

It was really dark now, the sky overcast and starless. I eased my legs slightly and felt the damp beginning to seep through my clothes. We were forced to rely on our hearing for indications of what was happening. It told us very soon that the man who walked with a limp was very close. The realisation drew us nearer in the gloom. There was something uncanny in that unnatural scuffling noise.

'Are we fools, or can it possibly be Rathmore?' I breathed.

Carol's face was touching mine. One strand of scented hair touched the back of my neck. It made me shiver suddenly.

'What are we going to do if it is?' she wanted to know.

I hadn't the faintest idea. 'Wait and see what happens,' I answered.

The man stopped short on the road below us. I don't think either of us expected that, and it came as something of a shock to our keyed-up nerves. For a moment there was no sound in the darkness, and then we heard the splutter of a match and saw the flame. His face was brought into sharp relief as he bent to light a cigarette.

It was Rathmore all right. There was no doubt about it, and I tried to work out how he knew where to be, and how he managed to get there at all. I gave up guessing. Rathmore coughed again, and leaned back in the shadows just below me. It was then that the dawn of a desperate scheme flashed through my mind. I kept very still for a second as it took shape. In my hand was the heavy jack handle I had brought from the Bentley. The head of our enemy was no more than three or four feet from where I was. By stretching out my arm, I could almost have touched his hair.

The temptation to put him out of the game was too great for me to resist, and I also had vague hopes of gaining something useful from my act. To lay the man out effectively called for great care, for I should have to strike quickly or not at all.

With the utmost caution, I moved fractionally nearer the edge of the bank and flexed my arm so that I had a clear field of movement.

Carol beside me was rigid, and I think she knew what I intended to do. I could hear her breath, the faintest murmur of tense intakes in the stillness around us. Her fingers touched my hand. The pressure spoke agreement. I was glad of that. For all I knew, I might be committing us to immediate danger.

By crawling inches I cased my arm free, gripping the length of metal tightly in my fingers. Now, I thought. My brain was an icy block inside my head. Prickles of excitement raced and played across the skin of my body.

I struck.

The shock of the blow jarred through my arm. I felt and heard the dull thud of metal striking bone. Rathmore grunted a little and Carol gasped. In an instant I was on my feet and jumping down into the road. I stumbled across the man's inert body and pitched forward on my hands. With a muttered curse, I was up again and groping in my pocket for the torch. I felt a strange elation at the success of my attack. Gaston's killer was in my power.

Rathmore lay quite still where he had fallen. In the light of the torch, his face was unpleasant, the lips drawn back in a grin of surprise and pain that must have frozen there when I hit him.

'Carol,' I said quietly, 'come down and give me a hand to lift him up.'

She slithered down with a rattle of stones and dislodged earth and stood beside me. 'Where are we going to put him?' she asked in a hushed voice.

'We'll drag him back to the car and tie him up first. I want to search him, for one thing, and then when he comes round we may get some information out of him. We'll go round by the road to the car — he's too heavy to get up the bank.'

Together we hauled his unconscious body along the lane to the Bentley's hiding place. Neither of us spoke again till we reached our haven, and then I bundled Rathmore over the side of the car and onto the back seat. He was completely out, and I wondered if I'd struck too hard and killed him. Not that I felt the least remorse at the thought, but it would mean he would be unable to tell us anything, and there was still a whole lot I wanted to know.

Carol got some wire from the locker, and I lashed his arms and legs securely, then we looked at each other in the gloom. Her eyes were bright and I gave her a smile.

With hurrying fingers, I ran through the pockets of the man's jacket and trousers. As various things came to light, I passed them over to Carol and continued the search. Chief among my finds was an automatic. With an immense feeling of comfort, I slipped it into my own pocket.

'That's the lot,' I said at last. 'Now let's see what we've got.'

I slid into the front seat beside her and turned on the dash-lamp. It threw a reddish glow across our knees, revealing the small collection of articles I had taken from Rathmore. They lay spread out on the lap of her skirt. One by one I picked them up and examined our finds. First was the familiar red of a driving licence issued in the name of Bernard Rathmore.

'That establishes his identity, anyway,' I said. 'The thing I want to know is *what* he is more than *who* he is.'

'This might help if I could read it,' she said. In her fingers was a small square of stiff blue card. On one face was printed the number 87, and on the reverse side some writing in German.

'Let's have a look,' I said quickly. My German was by no means good, but I could read enough to tell what it was. 'Do you realise who we've caught?' I asked excitedly. 'This is an old Gestapo identity card, and I've just had a brainwave. If I'm not very much mistaken, our friend here is a member of some secret society that's sprung up since the war ended with the idea of keeping the Nazi ideals alive. Look.' I picked up a passport from her lap. 'This is visaed for Spain, England and South America. I'll lay you any odds you like that Rathmore is here in England trying to get his hands on this cache for his precious hopefuls in Germany.'

'But surely he'd know where it was

hidden without going to all this trouble?'

'Not necessarily. It's quite on the cards that the gang who hid it when things became too hot were roped in without being able to pass on the details to anybody else for future use. Probably they're all dead now. That's how I see it, anyway.'

'Then if what you say is true, I suppose Lili Marlene, as you call him, is just a plain crook trying to pick up something he heard about by accident?'

'Most likely.' I nodded. 'The point is that if I'm right, we've got one bunch taped. I wonder if Rathmore had anyone else working with him? And how the devil did he manage to find his way here?'

'You'd better ask him when he comes round.'

'By the look of it, that might not be for quite a while,' I answered. 'Is there anything else interesting among his things?'

'Only this, but I can't make head or tail out of it.'

She handed me a piece of paper. I took it and studied it carefully, but could make no sense of it. All it consisted of was a meaningless series of figures and letters.

'Looks like code of some sort,' I said. 'We'd better keep it, whatever it is.' I slipped it into my pocket.

It was only then that I noticed the time. Engrossed in our capture and the things we'd found, both of us had forgotten about the rendezvous at the crossroads.

'It's five to eleven!' I said. 'We'd better go back to the bank if we want to see anything else.'

'Will Rathmore be all right?'

'He's not likely to run away,' I said with a grin, 'but I'll gag him just in case he wakes up and takes it into his head to shout before we get back.'

A few moments later, we were once more ensconced in our old hiding place above the road. Everything was deathly still, and I began to wonder if we could have missed the appointment. Apparently, however, it was the conspirators themselves who were late, because after a wait of some ten minutes we heard footsteps coming up from the direction of the village. Whether it was Lili Marlene or the so-called artist I could not be sure, but quite shortly the man came to a halt on the opposite side of the road.

We were not left long in doubt as to which of the two men it was. Very quietly he hummed to himself. A tune I well remembered.

10

Before I could made up my mind whether to take any action against the man or wait for further developments, I caught the sound of a car approaching the cross-roads. It suddenly came to me that if this was the artist with his Lanchester, we should be faced with the possibility of the two men carrying straight on to the cache without giving us a chance to follow or hear what was being said. When the car drew up, I realised my fears were well founded, and cursed myself for not foreseeing such an eventuality and taking steps to meet it.

The dark shape of the saloon loomed big in the narrow lane below us, and, after a muttered word, I heard the door open and then slam again. With a whine of gears, the car reversed and turned down the road that led past the spot at which the Bentley was hidden. We were alone; left standing at the post, as it were.

'Quick,' I said to Carol, 'we'll have to get the car and try to pick up their trail. They're heading for the coast.'

'Somewhere near where the cruiser is, I expect,' she answered as we began to run across the field.

'Why didn't I think of this before?' I muttered bitterly. 'We may have the devil of a chase now, and give ourselves away into the bargain.'

I started the car and sent it bumping and lurching out of the shallow pit in which it rested, swinging round to follow in the wake of the saloon. I dared not use any lights for fear they would be seen by our quarry, but had to rely entirely on the faintly reflected beam of the other car's lights as it travelled down the road ahead. Fortunately for us they seemed to be in no great hurry, or I could never have kept up. But as it was, I slowly managed to overhaul the Lanchester, keeping my distance when we were no more than a hundred yards behind it.

Where we were heading for I had very little notion, my sense of direction having quickly been upset by the many twists and turns of the lane we were following. Keeping in touch required all my concentration, so that although I felt sure it would be somewhere on the coast, there was nothing to indicate our exact destination, and when the driver of the saloon suddenly slowed down I was almost taken by surprise. Just before he came to a stop, however, I pulled up and cut the engine. In the ensuing silence I could hear the muffled throb of the saloon, and then that, too, ceased.

I was glad then for the fine drizzle of rain that had come on. Coupled with the general denseness of the night, it gave us reasonably effective concealment, for there was no other when I looked round. Had we been on the skyline, we must have been spotted; but though the road was straight, we had come to rest in a slight dip that was as black as ink and provided perfect cover.

I could just see the line of the hedge on my right. Slight noises came from the saloon; a door opened and shut; I heard the scrape of shoes on the road, then a creaking sound as if a gate was being pushed back. Almost at once the car started up again and turned off the road to the right.

'They've gone into a field,' I said quietly. 'We'll have to leave the car and follow on foot.'

As I spoke, I climbed down with Carol beside me. Together we moved cautiously up in the wake of the Lanchester. Sure enough, at the spot at which it had stopped was a gate standing wide open, and from this a narrow track stretched away to lose itself in the darkness.

I led the way through and watched the lurching beam of the headlights ahead as the car bounced along the rutted path. Presently it stopped again, but this time the driver turned the lights out and I could hear nothing after the slam of a door.

We hurried our steps then, for I did not want to be left too far behind and so lose all trace of our quarry. The going was tricky, and we had great difficulty in not making a noise, but at last we topped a crest and the track petered out on to smooth grassland. Here it was that the car had halted, and we passed it in the darkness.

At first I was uncertain which way to go, but once again Fate was kind. The sudden flash of a torch some fifty yards in front gave me the direction. By straining my eyes, I could just make out the skyline. Silhouetted against it were two dim figures that moved slowly till they disappeared down the slope of the hill on which we stood. From somewhere ahead came a soft murmur of whispering sound like the rustle of leaves in a breeze.

'The sea,' breathed Carol.

A moment later we heard it more clearly, and at the same time I saw two pin-pricks of light in the distance. 'That's probably the cruiser's riding lights,' I said. 'I wonder if they're making for that first, or going straight to the cache.'

'The cache,' she said. 'Look!'

She pointed away to the left, where I caught a glimpse of the bobbing flash of the torch again. It showed against a mass of shadow which till then I had been unable to identify, but now recognised as the grim shape of the old Martello tower we had noted on our first sight of Frigate's Hard earlier in the day.

'The stuffs probably hidden inside,' I whispered. 'Not a bad place to hide it either. Come on.'

We stumbled on through the blackness of night that pressed around us. I dare not use the torch, so we had to pick our way as best we could. Once I fell headlong into a ditch, and a few minutes after that Carol stifled a sudden cry of alarm as she blundered against the figure of a scarecrow that enfolded her horridly in its damp, limp arms.

The drizzle of rain came down more heavily. As a country ramble, that journey to the tower left much to be desired. I began to hate every yard of progress we made. The slope of the field was wet and slippery. Our feet skidded from under us as we slithered hand in hand. All the time we had to make as little noise as possible. The thing became a nightmare, that groping in the dark. And then we reached a point within twenty yards of our objective.

I stopped then and tried to make up my mind on the best line of action to take. Should we walk straight in and hold the two men up at the point of a gun, or wait till they came out with the treasure that had sent them there?

'Let's wait,' said Carol. I decided she was right. When they had the stuff, they would be less alert as well as having their hands full. Our chances of success would be far greater if we waited; besides which, by leaving them to it, they were doing the donkey work for us by unearthing the cache. If we did walk in, we had no idea of the exact hiding place in the old ruin, and they would hardly be likely to tell us if we asked.

Crouching down in the shadow of the tower that rose above us like a great black thundercloud, we listened intently to the little noises that came from inside the thick walls. I picked out the faint clatter of stones being moved, the sound of boots on gravel, muttering voices, and finally a faint cry of triumph, followed immediately by feverish activity as if the searchers had at last found what they wanted.

'Won't be long now!' I breathed cheerfully. 'How do you feel?'

'Scared stiff,' Carol answered.

I put my arm round her waist. 'After the treasure, then Antoine,' I whispered. 'If we can find him, that is. I wonder where this madness is leading us.'

I felt her shiver against me, but she said nothing. Up above our heads yawned the deeper black of the entrance to the tower. We had placed ourselves on the right of it so as to be in the best position for our attack when Lili and the artist attempted to come out. They would have to drop a matter of five feet from the door to the ground, and that, I decided, would be my chance. When the moment for action came, I intended to push Carol behind me so that she would be out of danger if there was any shooting. I hoped, however, that it would not come to that, and felt that if I could effect enough surprise it would be needless. The birds would fall into our hands without serious trouble.

So I thought and so I hoped as we waited there in the blind darkness, our nerves taut and keyed up till we heard and saw things that were not there to hear or see. I am never likely to forget those dragging seconds that stretched into aching minutes. They seemed then to be filled with menace and danger, and yet I felt confident that our task would be easy.

At that time, I don't think I realised all the difficulties that might present themselves. I gave no thought as to how we were to hold our captives once we had them in our power. The fact that they were there almost in our hands was enough, but I wonder now what would have happened if we had taken them both prisoner. Back in the Bentley we already had Rathmore, trussed up and probably conscious again by now. It never struck me as difficult then that I was proposing to make a further addition to our haul. True, I had a gun, but there was still so much I did not know that even if I caught Lili Marlene and the artist I doubt if I should have been much nearer the solving of the mystery.

Fate, however, with the help of the late German espionage system, had dealt the cards; and had I known it then, the play was to be of a different nature to the way I had planned it.

Exactly how long we waited I don't know, but there came a moment when I heard footsteps approaching the entrance from the inside, and tensed myself for action. I was a little worried by the fact that there appeared to be only one man about to come out of the tower, and wondered what would happen when his companion heard the noise of my attack on him.

Even as I turned the thought over in my mind, he spoke in the darkness above us. I could picture him standing there in the opening of the door, pausing long enough to say what he wanted over his shoulder before dropping down to the ground.

'Get the stuff clear,' he said. 'I'm going down to collect Perigrin from the boat — we'll need his help to shift it from here. If you try any tricks on your own, I'll get you before you cover a mile. Understand?'

I recognised the voice as that of Lili Marlene. There was a muffled grunt of agreement from the interior, and then with a light thud the speaker landed close behind us on the soggy ground.

I did some quick thinking. Carol and I pressed back against the wall. Having heard what he said, I changed my mind about holding the man up, for I realised it would be foolish. If I allowed him to continue on his way, we should only have the artist to deal with in the tower, and then we could take Lili and his henchman, Perigrin, on their return.

With hurrying footsteps and the wavering light of his torch gleaming in front of him, Lili set off in the direction of the shore. He gave no sign that he suspected our presence, for which blessing I was glad, and when all sound of his progress had faded away in the distance I stood up very quietly.

With the utmost caution, I began to climb up to the door above me. I wanted to see what the man inside was engaged on before I did anything rash. I had one foot on a protruding brick in the face of the wall when things started to happen with dreadful suddenness.

Even as my hand reached out to grope for the opening of the door, there came a faint hissing noise from the inner darkness of the tower. For an instant I listened to it, unable to connect it with anything; and then, before I could make another move to peer through the door, the curious sound was drowned and flooded out by the most fearful scream I ever wished to hear.

Mingled with the agonised cry was the noise of a body thrashing and beating in unbearable pain. With a sudden sense of premonition, I wriggled up and stared down into the gloomy interior of the place, lighting it with my torch as I did so.

The sight that met my eyes transfixed me with horror and fascination. For a moment I remained absolutely still, gazing at the scene before me.

Carol scrambled up beside me then. I heard her gasp of breath as she saw what I was looking at.

'Oh God,' she moaned fearfully. 'What is it?'

I found my voice at last. It sounded harsh and dry.

'Orange Death,' I muttered. 'Remember Gaston's warning?'

11

Peering down into the well of shadow that enveloped the interior of the tower, I felt shaken and sick. It was all so fantastic, yet so horribly real. There before my eyes lay the artist, or perhaps I should say what was left of him. Never having seen the man's face, I doubt if I should have recognised him anyway; but even if I had known him, there would have been little chance of identifying him now.

His face, his head, and the whole of the upper part of his body was a mass of yellow coloured foam that bubbled and seethed on his skin like a million moving insects crawling interminably one upon the other.

The man himself was absolutely still and silent, and I knew without telling that he was dead. What fiendish trick had been used to guard the hoard of Nazi treasure I could only guess, but that it had been effective was all too obvious. Overall there rose the awful stench of acid-charred flesh, while a faint haze of heavy vapour still drifted about the agony-twisted corpse.

The dreadful Orange Death had done its work well, and from a point in the wall just above the spot at which the man had been working came a trickle of the filthy stuff as the container dribbled the last of its contents down the tough bricks to gather in a shallow pool of foaming horror on the uneven floor.

Thinking back, I remembered the hissing noise that had immediately preceded the scream of the dead man, guessed that that must have been the moment when he had sprung the trap that was to cause his death in such a ghastly manner.

How long we stood there in the deep recess of the old door, I don't pretend to know. There was something so petrifying about the scene that only when I suddenly felt Carol sway against me did I come to my senses.

'Steady,' I said. 'There's nothing we can do here.'

I turned and dropped to the ground, raising my arms and lifting her down beside me. She shuddered as she stood close in the darkness, gripping my arm in a tight, panicky grasp of horror.

'What . . . what was it?' she gasped at last. Her face was lifted to mine in the gloom. Somehow the sight of it, dim as it was, brought reality near again.

'Some diabolical trick that was meant to protect the cache from anyone who didn't know about it,' I said. 'Apparently Gaston only told them half the secret, or maybe they didn't wait to hear it all. Anyway, treasure or not, I'm not going in there until it's light and I can see what I'm up against — there may be some more of those jolly little 'fire extinguisher' affairs dotted about for, all we know.'

We were standing beneath the frowning mass of the tower, talking in low tones. There was no need for such silence, I suppose, but somehow I hated the idea of raising my voice above a mutter in that place that was so close to death.

I took Carol's arm and led her some yards away. I wanted time to think and work out our next move. Should we, I wondered, try to seize Lili Marlene on his way back from the boat, or stay where we were till he returned? In the end I decided in favour of the latter course, since I could not be sure of the exact path the man would come by. Added to that was the fact that Perigrin would be coming with him, and to hold up two men on a pitch-dark night in country I did not know seemed to offer far too many opportunities for counter moves by the enemy. When we had them safe, it would be time enough to have a look at the cruiser and see if it contained anything interesting. I came to the conclusion that it was probably no more than a means of transport for the treasure they hoped to obtain, but there was so much uncertainty about the whole affair that I should not have felt satisfied until I had examined it.

It also struck me as a possible hiding place for Antoine. Seeing that we had no idea where he was, it would be foolish to overlook the one that was handiest, for he could well have been held a captive in the boat itself.

I knew now that everything rested on finding him and freeing him. If I failed in that, I should fail in discovering all the other facts of the mystery that still remained to be solved. The riddle of Christine and the sapphire ring, for instance; and the strange way in which Gaston appeared to be linked with Antoine himself. There was so much I wanted to know, and as far as I could see there was only one way of finding it out — by finding Antoine and making him talk, either willingly or under pressure.

We did not have long to wait before there came the sound of hurried footsteps and the flashing beam of a torch. A moment later, I made out the forms of two men coming towards us.

Gripping the gun tightly in my hand, I prepared to meet them, thrusting Carol behind me as I stood up from where we had been crouching together.

Almost on top of us, they blundered closer. Lili Marlene was speaking in a worried voice.

'Funny,' he said, 'I could have sworn I heard a cry back there. Hope the fool hasn't hurt himself or anything. We've had quite enough hold-ups in this business already.'

It was just then that I confronted Mm, switching on my torch as I walked forward, blinding Mm with its sudden light. 'He's hurt himself, all right!' I said grimly. 'And what's more, this is another hold-up for you. You'll get hurt as well if you don't put your hands up — both of you!'

For a moment I thought he was going to spring at me. My finger tightened instinctively on the trigger. Just in time to save his life, he relaxed and stood still.

'Who the devil do you think you are?' he demanded fiercely, but his hands crept upwards in spite of his bluster.

'You should know me by now,' I snapped. 'Your pal Coolis tried to kill me last night, for one thing. He's dead now, I gather. So is your tame artist friend.' I jerked my head towards the tower. 'And so will you be if you're not careful.' I stopped and called to Carol. 'Search them for weapons,' I told her, 'but for heaven's sake keep out of my line of fire — this thing's liable to go off suddenly.'

With deft fingers, she ran through their pockets, producing a second automatic from Lili's coat, but nothing more lethal than a jack-knife from Perigrin. 'That's the lot,' she said. 'What now?'

'We'll show them what happened to their partner,' I replied.

At the point of the gun, I jabbed Lili forward towards the door of the tower, while Carol treated Perigrin in the same way. I think both men realised they were in a dangerous position, and we made it abundantly clear that the slightest trick would end in instant death for the one who tried it.

Jumping down into the well of the tower, Lili stared in fascination at the body of the artist. It was a gruesome enough sight and did little to improve the nerves of Perigrin, who began to speak excitedly in some language I failed to understand. Lili ordered him to shut up, then turned to face me in the light of the torch.

'Well,' he said flatly, 'what exactly do you want? A share? Say, forty-sixty?'

'That won't wash, my friend,' I replied. 'You're not going to lay hands on that stuff at all, for one thing. And for another, I want to know where Antoine is.'

'If I tell you, do we go free?'

'That depends on a number of things,' I replied carefully. 'You're in no position to bargain.'

I certainly had no intention of letting the men go free, but it seemed polite to give them some grounds for supposing that I might. 'Where's your prisoner, first of all?' I asked again. 'When I know that, I may be prepared to talk.'

'On the boat.' His answer was sulky and grudging.

'Good. In that case, you will walk in front of us back to my car. There's someone there already who might be pleased to see you.'

'Who's that?'

'An old friend of yours, I believe. Get moving!'

We must have made a strange procession as we wended our way up the long sloping meadow to where the track began, then down it to the road. Halting

156

at last beside the Bentley, I told Carol to bind our two prisoners with wire while I held them covered with both guns. Not until then did I turn on the light and reveal the face of Rathmore staring up at us with malicious eyes from his place on the back seat of the car. He was fully conscious now and, if looks were anything to go by, in the worst sort of mood a man can well suffer.

'I believe you two know each other,' I said somewhat sarcastically as I jabbed Lili in the ribs and indicated that he should get in beside Rathmore.

'How do you expect me to get in there with my legs tied?' he snarled.

'Then fall in!' I retorted, giving him a push that sent him toppling over the side to fall across Rathmore.

'Now you!' I ordered Perigrin. He failed to understand, so I treated him in the same way. The back of the Bentley now presented a strange sight. It seemed to be full of arms and legs and sullen expressions. I nearly laughed aloud till I remembered what desperate men we were dealing with. The slightest relaxation on my part, and they would have no hesitation in killing us both as soon as look at us; and what was just as likely, kill each other as well. At least, I felt sure Rathmore and Lili would try it. That they hated each other was clear to the dimmest intelligence, and to leave them together was foolish. I could see nothing else for it, however; and when it appeared as if everything was well under control, I took Carol with me and we struck off in the direction of the shore.

It did not take us long to locate the dinghy in which Perigrin had come ashore; and, scuffing out to where the lights of the cruiser showed on the dark water, we scrambled aboard. Dropping down into the well and opening the door of the cabin, I soon found Antoine. He was stretched out on a bunk and firmly tied up with ropes. His clothes were muddy and bedraggled, while on his hands I saw a number of small burn marks that gave me cause to think. I had expected him to be bound, but the thing that rather took me by surprise was the fact that he was unconscious. I hadn't reckoned on that, and we had to lift his dead weight over the side into the dinghy. From what I could see, I guessed he must have been doped, for there were no signs of violence on his head or elsewhere on his body apart from the burn scars.

In silence we rowed back to the shore, our minds busy with the crowded developments of the last few minutes. I felt that now at last we were on the verge of solving the whole mystery, and somehow the realisation elated me after all that had gone before. I felt, too, that I had had my fill of excitement for the time being, and should be almost glad to continue my broken journey to New-castle. How little I knew then that the thing was far from being over; that before another hour was out we should be facing danger again in the dark of the night, and that events were shaping themselves to an end that had never entered our heads.

I realised, too, as we moved across the water to the shallow line of surf ahead, that as soon as I could I should be forced to report all that had happened to the police, handing over our prisoners and telling the authorities where the treasure was hidden. The affair had gone too far, and ended in such a way that I should find myself in queer street if I attempted to hide any longer all that had occurred.

My best plan, I decided, was to motor straight up to London and deliver my charges to Scotland Yard as being the most direct method of bringing to the notice of the right people the incredible circumstances in which we had found the cache, for I knew it was connected with something that was outside the normal jurisdiction of the ordinary police.

As I dragged the boat up the beach clear of the waves and lifted Antoine's limp body from it, I told Carol of my decision, and she gave her ready consent. Whatever Antoine had to tell us, I must do as I had said. Even if the exposure of the whole thing brought unwanted publicity and the loss of his valuables, it could no longer be avoided.

'What are we going to do with Antoine?' she asked as I dumped him on the sand. 'We can't carry him all the way to the car, can we?'

'No. You'd better stay here with him while I go and fetch the car as near as I can get it. It'll give me a chance to see if the hornet's nest in the back is still alive, too. Don't move from here under any circumstances. I won't be longer than I can help.'

With that I headed inland, and before many minutes were over arrived at the car again. It stood just as I had left it, but as I drew nearer I became aware of some subtle difference about the outline of its lean, familiar shape. With quickening steps I covered the remaining distance, coming to an abrupt halt as I saw the cause of the illusion.

The car was the same all right, but now there was an addition to it that made my blood run cold, and beads of sweat start clammily on my forehead.

12

Sick with dread, I crept nearer till I was standing right in front of the radiator, staring at what had once been Rathmore.

His body was tied spread-eagle across the top of the bonnet, lashed down from one mudguard to the other. But it was not so much his unnatural position that shocked me as the way in which he had come to die.

He lay on his back. Sticking up at an acute angle from the slight mound of his stomach was the handle of a long screwdriver I always carried in the tool-box. Nor was that the worst part. With a sudden feeling of utter revulsion, I realised his face was brutally disfigured, though whether that had been done while he still lived or not I could not tell.

The savagery of the act, and the cold-bloodedness of this murder, sent a shiver through my frame. I wanted to turn and run from the scene of horror that was before me. The whole air and atmosphere of its barbarity seemed to pervade the place. I saw a trickle of blood coursing down the sleek side of the bonnet; one partly detached eye dangling loose, a horrid orb, on the sweat-streaked cheek. I think I must have come near to fainting at that moment, probably for the first time in my life. A maze of desperate questions flooded over me; my brain refused to function, becoming instead a whirl of fearful fantasy. What could I do? Or say? I felt numb at the stark evidence that lay before me. Like a drunken man, I reeled against the friendly support of the radiator, frantically trying to think clearly, and failing miserably.

In sheer desperation, I pulled myself erect and cautiously moved round the car till I was level with the back seat. It was only then that I realised there was no sign of either of the other two men who had so recently been captive there. I saw their tangled bonds, and the pair of pliers with which they must have freed themselves, but of the men there was not the slightest trace. They were gone.

For some time, it didn't dawn on me that there was danger in the very fact of their disappearance. All I knew was that I was alone with the horribly mutilated corpse of Rathmore, and that to move it I had to untie it from the bonnet of my car. I didn't look forward to that. It filled me with dismay, but I knew there was nothing else for it, and set myself to face the gruesome task.

Hardly had I begun to untwist the first strand of wire that held Rathmore in place before some sixth sense warned me that I was no longer alone on the scene of the crime. With a prickle of fear, I ceased my efforts and stood rigid, grasping the gun in my hand and ready for instant action.

At that moment I cursed the darkness that made me as good as blind. I wanted to thrust it aside; to call out to the unseen man to show himself. I wanted to hide myself completely; to make myself a part of the deepest shadows. Had I thought about it long enough, I should have realised that I was just as invisible as the other. My torch was out and I crouched down behind the massive bulk of the car. No one could have picked me out as being a separate entity. My nerves, already unstrung by discovery of the body of Rathmore, were now at breaking point. An unreasoning fear took hold of me. The slightest whisper of stealthy movement behind my back sent me whirling round in a cold sweat of terror.

'Who's there?' I gasped.

My eyes were burning with the strain of trying to see in the blackness. There was no answer. Nothing came back at me but the faint murmur of the distant sea and the uneven drip of rain from laden bushes. Only mockery lived in the silent, laughing shadows. I shivered. My voice sounded unnaturally loud. Danger stood close; I knew it, but that was all. Where, or how, or when, I had no means of telling.

I cursed myself for speaking. It would have given my position away, and now the lurking menace in the night would strike; strike and kill me from an angle I could not guess.

Very slowly I turned right round,

searching everywhere for any sign of sound or movement. As long as I live, I shall never forget the tension of those awful minutes. If I walked away, I expected a fusillade of shots to hammer into me; yet if I stayed where I was, I dreaded to think what might even then be creeping up on me from the dark pall around. In the vividness of my imagination, I could almost feel the cold steel of a knife thrusting between my ribs as something sprang at me too late to avoid. I lived then in a ghastly nightmare, made worse by my very ignorance of its nature.

Again came the faintest murmur of sibilant sound somewhere in front of me. My scalp crawled icily with fear, yet no longer could I bear to wait for the terror to materialise and strike. I had to know what shape it took; I had to grapple with it; to feel my fingers sinking into something tangible that I could touch and hold and kill before it did the same to me.

What courage I had left was hi shreds. I tried to pull myself together and think clearly. Reason at last told me that if Lili and his henchmen were going to attack me, I need have no fear of their being armed with guns, since we had disarmed them. The thought gave me some small comfort. It gave me, too, courage that I badly needed.

With the utmost caution, I crept in the direction of the sound I had heard. Ought I to shine my torch? I might be able to see what lurked in my path before it saw me. Slowly I swung the flash-lamp round till it was facing the place from which, a near as I could judge, the sound had come.

Uncertain what to expect, I pressed the switch and sent its beam flooding away into the shadows, tearing away their shroud, revealing stark outlines and sodden leaves. Nothing stirred.

I swept the light further round, my eyes fixing on the bright shifting circle of golden radiance. Deathly stillness clamped down like a stiff blanket. What was I doing? I asked myself. Was I asking for sudden death? Was I imagining things? No longer could I answer for the steadiness of my nerves; they were ragged and frayed with the strain of waiting and listening.

And then the silence was broken. I

heard the sound of a foot crushing grit behind me. Too late, I spun round. An upraised arm came sweeping down at me. Something struck my head with blinding force. The world seemed to dissolve in a sparkling shower of red and yellow lights. I went out . . .

When I opened my eyes again, I was lying on wet grass, and the dark figure of a man loomed black above me. I felt sick and my head was spinning.

'So you've woken up at last!' The voice was Lili's, and the knowledge did little to reassure me. I struggled into a sitting position and glared at him.

'Well,' I said as steadily as I could, 'what do you want now that I'm awake?'

'Where's the woman?' he rasped.

'I left her in the boat,' I lied. 'We found Antoine, but couldn't move him on our own — not all the way back to the car.'

'Good. In that case, we can carry on. You're going to help me transfer the stuff from the tower to the cruiser. After that, we shall see what happens.'

'Where's your own man?' I asked.

'Perigrin? He got himself killed by

Rathmore before I could handle the situation.' He paused. 'Rathmore paid for that,' he added reflectively.

'Yes, so I noticed,' I said acidly. 'I wish you hadn't left your handiwork all over my car.'

'That should worry you — you won't be wanting it again.' His look was baleful. Then he kicked me hard in the ribs. 'Get up! I've wasted enough time on you already.' Under the menace of his gun, I got slowly to my feet.

'March!' he ordered. 'And I advise you not to try anything foolish. I shan't have the slightest compunction in killing you if you do.'

I quite believed him. 'All right,' I said. 'I'll behave myself — I'm too fond of living not to.'

Strangely enough, I didn't feel so frightened now that I knew what I was up against. At least he wasn't going to kill me immediately, and before anything else could happen there was always a chance that things might shape themselves very differently.

Submissively, I began to walk in front

of him towards the tower, frantically turning all kinds of fantastic plans over in my mind as we went. In actual fact, I think I was far more worried about Carol than I was about myself. What would happen to her if Lili discovered her whereabouts, I dreaded to think. I didn't like the idea of her falling into his hands at all. Suddenly her safety became the most important thing in my life. I knew I didn't want to lose her; that if I did, nothing else would ever matter again. And yet what could I do?

The situation seemed desperate. I turned again to find some way of thwarting my captor. I was to be used as a means of carrying the treasure that had already cost five men their lives. Unless I could do something about it, it looked as if it was very shortly going to take toll of my own as well. That mustn't happen; for Carol's sake that mustn't happen.

I toyed with the idea of falling down and tripping Lili in the hope that I should regain the gun in the ensuing mêlée. Almost as soon as I thought of it, however, I discarded it as being too risky.

He would probably shoot me before I could do anything.

Without my being able to work out any suitable plan of action, we arrived at the tower. In silence, Lili motioned me to go through the door and down into the well of the interior. In the beam of his torch I could see where I was, but even more clearly he could see me, and once inside he lit a storm lantern as well.

I hated the idea of approaching the mass of yellow foam that still covered the artist, but he thrust me forward from behind. 'Go on, or I'll push you into it!' he snapped.

Reluctantly I did as he said, stepping across the corpse to the wall where he had been working. I saw then that his efforts had opened up a square recess in the brickwork just below the wet nozzle of the container that had held the Orange Death.

The smell was awful. I barely stopped myself from retching. There was something hideous about the whole place. It stank of murder and the hand of terror.

On Lili's order, I delved into the hole

and fetched out the first of the articles that rested within. What the hoard was worth in actual money value I never found out, but it made an impressive enough sight as I brought it to light piece by piece.

There were ingots of gold as well as silver. Some smaller bars I identified as platinum, and a leather bag that felt as if it contained stones. There must have been hundreds in it. Finally came a heavy canvas case I was barely able to lift.

For several minutes I worked feverishly under the man's guidance and the threat of the gun that never left my back for an instant. When there was nothing more to feel inside the hiding place I told him so, and with a satisfied grunt he stood back and motioned me to carry the stuff to the centre of the room.

'There's enough in that bag of stones alone to keep me in luxury for the rest of my days,' he said.

'Why did you bother to bring me along to get it out for you?' I demanded. 'You could easily have done it yourself in stages.'

'For the pleasure of seeing you squirm before you die.' He gave a humourless laugh at the dawning fear in my eyes.

'What are you going to do?'

'This,' he rasped.

Before I could move an inch, his foot caught me in the stomach, and the next instant I was spinning backwards towards the horrid yellow shape that had been the artist. I landed with a thud that partly winded me, to find my hands embedded in the sticky softness of the dead man's body.

For one terrible second I braced myself to accept the inevitable. I was going to burn and die in the same horrible fashion. I think I must have screamed at that moment. I heard a laugh echo eerily round the circular tower. It sounded thin and high-pitched. It was Lili, I knew. And then I realised something else. I wasn't burning. There was nothing more unpleasant about the stuff on my hands than a slight tingling sensation like a weak electric shock.

My heart leaped with the most wonderful relief I have ever known. There could only be one answer: the Orange

Death lost its power of destruction shortly after being exposed to the air.

But, if the wicked foam was dead, Lili and his gun remained just as great a menace as ever. I began to count the seconds that must separate me from the murder I read in his cold grey eyes. He, too, realised that nothing was happening to me where I lay half across the body of his late partner.

If I moved I should feel the bullet; if I stayed where I was, gazing up at him, I should feel it just as quickly. The suspense grew till I could hardly prevent myself jumping up and rushing him. Should I stand a chance, I wondered, if I made a scramble for it? The odds seemed too heavy. All I saw clearly was the black-circled muzzle of his gun. It grew enormous in my distorted vision; almost it covered the whole of the place, covered it in a yawning darkness. In fascinated horror I watched, unable to take my eyes from its cold magnet of shadow, the shadow of death.

Like a great dark lens it came closer, forcing me back till my head touched the ground. And then the spell was snapped by the sound of his voice. Hateful as it was, I felt as if the words brought me reason again.

'You're going to be lucky!' he whispered. 'Lucky to die quickly instead of like that.' He made a slight gesture towards the body that formed my pillow.

'Damn you!' I muttered wildly. 'Why kill me?'

'You signed your own death warrant by interfering. You can shut your eyes if you like.'

There was a taunting mockery in his last words that made me sick with apprehension.

'Damn you!' I breathed again. I felt like choking. It all seemed so useless and senseless. Was I going to lie there and be killed in cold blood without lifting a hand to defend myself? I made a slight movement, my eyes still fixed on the gun that never wavered.

'Now!' Lili's voice was utterly toneless, like a judge announcing sentence.

Instinctively, I closed my eyes to shut out the sight of that ring of metal. I didn't want to see its vicious spurt of livid flame; I didn't want to see death come at me from that fatal shadow.

In a sweat of terror, I tried to roll away from the arc of danger. Before I could cover an inch, the whole interior of the place reverberated with the crash of the report. Its hollow thud beat against the walls, racing back and forth from one side to the other in a million echoes.

I dreaded the tearing pain I expected, but there wasn't any. I just lay very still. For one instantaneous space of crawling time, I couldn't understand it. And then I knew I must be alive. The thought left me weak, hi my nostrils was the same stench that had been there all the time, but now there was another smell mingled with it. The tang of cordite and gun smoke awoke me from the paralysis of fear in which I lay.

Stretched on the floor beside me was the body of Lili Marlene. The gun lay loose in his fingers. I don't quite know what I expected to see when I looked round. What I did see was the dim silhouette of Carol standing in the doorway.

She cried out to me then. I think she thought I was dead until she saw me move. In a moment she was jumping down and running across the floor towards me. Seconds later I was holding her tightly in my arms, whispering jumbled words of wonder and relief.

I felt unsteady and badly shaken, but happier than I ever believed a man could be. Her lips were soft and warm, moist like a child's, hungrily demanding. The love that neither of us had recognised during the dark hours of haunting night suddenly found expression; found it in long minutes of magic that drove the nightmare we'd lived into forgotten limbo. Her supple body, lithe and yielding in my arms, took the place of everything else. For all the treasure of Croesus, for all the treasure that lay at our very feet, I would not have exchanged those precious moments.

13

'How did you get here?' I asked at last. There was much I failed to understand. The miracle of her arrival was uppermost in my mind.

'When you were gone a long time,' she answered, 'I decided to come and meet you. I know you told me not to move, but I couldn't help feeling uneasy, so I came. Then I heard voices in the tower and crept close enough to find out what was going on. You know the rest.'

'You were only just in time, my darling,' I said. 'Five seconds more and you'd have been a widow before we married!' I laughed then, my mood elated. Her mouth was sweet to kiss. 'What about Antoine?' I said, remembering the man. 'Is he still out for the count?'

She nodded. 'He was when I left him. We'd better go and fetch him, hadn't we?'

'Yes. We'll get the car nearer first and load all this stuff up as well — can't very well leave it for anyone else to pick up, can we?'

Together we started off for the track that led into the field. I refused to let her come right up to the Bentley with me, for I knew there was still my Unfinished task of removing Rathmore from the bonnet to be completed.

When it was done and his body laid out by the side of the road, I called her. She caught her breath when she saw the ominous shape near the car, but after a brief word of explanation I hurried her in and started up.

The job of transferring the load of treasure from the tower to the Bentley was no light one, but in the end we managed it successfully. And then, with Antoine's insensible body settled as comfortably as possible on the back seat, I turned and headed for the London road.

We were passing through Chelmsford when sounds of movement from the rear told us Antoine was recovering his senses. I pulled into the roadside and gave him a drink from the flask I carried. With dazed eyes, he stared from one to the other of us as if hardly believing what he saw.

'Feeling better?' I asked cheerfully.

For a moment he made no answer, then passed a hand across his forehead and slowly sat up straight. Only then did he seem to recognise Carol, and a faint smile showed on his lips at sight of her face.

'Thank you, yes, *mon ami*. I do not know what has been happening, but I feel I must owe you my life.' He spoke perfect English with only the merest trace of an accent.

'Don't try talking too much yet,' I advised him. 'Relax a bit and get your strength back first. We're on our way to Scotland Yard with the whole story — and the treasure. If you feel like it, you can tell us your part as we go.'

'Scotland Yard!' he repeated in something like dismay.

'Why not?' I retorted suspiciously. I didn't like the way he echoed the name. Had he too much to hide to risk an enquiry? I wondered. The thought wasn't going to stop me in my purpose anyhow.

He leaned forward over the back of my seat. 'You are groping about in the dark,' he said quietly.

I gave a rather hollow laugh at that. How right he was! Even now I was still too uncertain of myself to be sure of anything, apart from the fact that to my mind, the whole of England seemed to be littered with dead bodies, all of which were surrounded in a fog of mystery.

'I may be groping in the dark, m'sieu,' I replied, 'but I think it's high time this matter was brought to the notice of the police. It's already gone too far for my liking.' I paused. 'We shall probably all end up in prison for our pains, but that can't be helped. What objection can you possibly have to my decision?'

'Hear what I have to say first.' There was a quality of quiet authority in his voice that made the man somehow impressive despite his haggard and dishevelled appearance. For a moment I remained silent, but Carol stepped in before I could make up my mind what to say.

'Please tell us all you know,' she said.

'There's so much we don't understand.'

I switched off the engine at that, and waited for him to speak. There could be no harm in listening, I decided. It would clear up a lot and make things easier to explain when I reached London.

'All right,' I said. 'But make it as short as you can.'

'First of all,' he said, 'this matter in which you have become involved is not a thing for the police.'

'Why not?' I asked dryly. 'To my certain knowledge, there have already been six deaths since I myself came into it. Heaven knows how many more there might have been before that. If you don't consider that a matter for the police, I do!'

'From your point of view, *mon ami*, yes; but not from mine. At least not yet.'

'Go on,' I said resignedly. 'I'm prepared to listen.'

He smiled then, and the twinkle in his eyes was infectious. I found I was warming to the plump little Frenchman in spite of myself.

'You must understand first of all that I

am not all I seem to be,' he began. 'Besides being a wine importer, as I have no doubt Carol has already told you, I have been working for many years for the Intelligence Service of the French Republic in conjunction with your own British government.'

He paused while we digested this news. I must admit that any doubts I had about his integrity were allayed by the announcement, while Carol gave a little gasp of amazement. He seemed pleased with the effect of his words, and quickly went on: 'How much you two know, or have discovered, I am ignorant, but for the purpose of explaining things I will assume it is nothing.'

'It amounts to very little more than that,' I put in ruefully. 'We've guessed a good deal, but that's all.'

'For a long time we have known of the existence of a secret store of money and valuables hidden in England,' he said. 'It was collected by the Nazis against the time when they would need ready funds to pay their agents in the event of war with your country.'

'So you told Carol the truth about that part of it?'

'Yes, I did. It was impossible to tell her the whole of the story at the time for a number of reasons, but that I felt she could know without harm. The rest I had to make up to fit the facts well enough to explain my actions. However, to continue. Though we knew about this hoard, we could not locate it. It was a matter that was of importance to both our countries, and more so when war broke out, as you can well imagine. For a long time we were unrewarded, but eventually, after several years' work, poor Gaston traced it.'

'*Poor* Gaston!' Both Carol and I echoed the words in unison.

He nodded. 'Yes. He was my right-hand man during the whole of the assignment. We began working together as far back as 1938, though I knew him long before that.'

The news stunned me. It upset all the ideas I had built up and brought things tumbling about my ears.

'But,' I stammered, 'from what I gathered, he robbed you and was no better than a common-or-garden thief! I hardly know what to think.'

Antoine grinned. 'Patience, *mon ami,*' he laughed. 'We were forced to resort to all kinds of subterfuge in order to achieve our purpose. It was known that large quantities of stolen property were finding their way to the hiding place, and our robbery was carefully planned to see if it was not possible for Gaston's haul to follow it. At our first attempt, we were entirely unsuccessful. My valuables were passed on by Gaston through channels we suspected. But unfortunately he was unable to trace them beyond the second pair of hands through which they passed. You can imagine our chagrin!'

He spread his hands in a continental gesture of dismay. I couldn't help grinning at his mobile face as he peered at us in the gloom.

'We tried the same trick in England,' he continued, 'and for a time it seemed as if we had again failed. But it was not so. A few days ago I heard from Gaston. I knew then that he had found what we wanted.'

'We found the note,' I put in. 'I'm

185

afraid the whole thing seemed most suspicious to me at the time, and the letter was couched in strange terms.'

'We were doing strange things,' he said with a laugh. 'Anyhow, it was impossible for me to keep the appointment with him, and as you know, I sent Carol. I expected no more than details of where the store was hidden, so that she could well act as a messenger without even knowing what vital information she was carrying. As I saw it, there was no danger in the mission at all. How deeply I regret my foolishness in sending her, I can only tell you. You will understand my feelings.'

'Quite,' I replied dryly. 'Things went wrong with a vengeance. You yourself were tricked pretty neatly, I suppose?'

'In the simplest possible manner. A phone message to say that Carol was injured and would I come immediately. I walked straight into the arms of a man named Coolis. Before I realised what was happening, I was kidnapped!'

'Who exactly was Coolis?' I asked.

'An international crook who had been working on similar lines to our own,' he replied. 'How he found out about Gaston I cannot tell, but that he did is clear. What he did not know was his whereabouts. I was bundled into a car, and once inside compelled to give them the information they required.'

'A Mercedes?'

He nodded. 'Yes. They tortured me with burning cigarette ends until I spoke; and then we drove to York.'

'Just a minute,' I cut in. 'That car passed us on the road and I was shot at by someone inside it. It was only sheer luck that we weren't both killed. How on earth did they know we were a potential danger to their plans?'

He pulled a face at my words. 'That, I fear, was my own fault. Just as we were overtaking your car, I made an attempt to attract attention. I did not know, of course, whose car it was. I merely wanted to let someone know I was in danger. However, just as we came up behind, I recognised Carol in the beam of the headlights. Before I could stop myself, I called out her name. I could have bitten off my tongue for doing it, but by then it was too late. They put two and two together and guessed you were also on your way to York. The rest you know.

'From York we drove south again. It was then that the accident occurred in which Coolis was killed. How the other man and I escaped, I do not know. It was a miracle. We were thrown clear, right over a hedge, and luckily for me, both landed in a pond. I suppose that saved our lives. I was bound and could do nothing to help myself, but he pulled me out and made me walk across country for hours. My identity papers he took and left on Coolis's body before we left the scene of the wreck. Finally he stole another car and continued on his way, taking me with him. Somewhere on the coast, I was transferred to the boat on which you found me. He left me in charge of a person called Perigrin, and it was he who doped me to save himself the trouble.'

He stopped and lit a cigarette. Then: 'That is all I can tell you, my friend. But you will see that it is most important for me to get in touch with my own headquarters before going to the police.'

'Who was Rathmore?' I asked. I wanted to know all there was to know about the affair.

'He was the agent of a secret society that was seeking to perpetuate Nazi ideals,' he explained. 'They needed funds, and the hoard was an obvious place to obtain them. The trouble was that all traces of it had been lost when the men responsible for it were captured as spies during the war.'

'I guessed as much,' I answered. 'Oh, and speaking of Rathmore, I found this code work in his pocket. You'd better take charge of it, I think — it seems to be up your street more than mine.'

His face lit up when he saw the slip of paper with its figures and letters. That it must be important I could tell at a glance. His next words proved it.

'But this is marvelous,' he gasped. 'This is the key we have sought for months. Now we shall be able to crush this menace before it grows!' He gave an excited laugh.

'Well,' I said, 'I'm glad to hear that. You've certainly cleared up a lot of things

I didn't understand, but there are still one or two problems left. What's been worrying both Carol and me is the connection between herself and Gaston. She knows nothing about it, and until yesterday didn't even know that she was your godchild. Nor, for that matter, that she was also the mysterious Christine. If you could explain those things for us, we'd both be grateful.'

He seemed slightly abashed at our unearthing of that part of the affair, but went on readily enough, speaking direct to Carol rather than to me. 'Francois Gaston,' he began, 'though a true Frenchman and possessed of a great heart, was at times a very strange man. I had the highest regard for him in spite of his many faults, and am deeply sorry that he died the way he did. As you seem to have discovered, there was a link between you and this man about which you know nothing. Allow me to explain.

'Many years ago, Carol, I had a niece. She was a lovely creature, and watching her grow to womanhood was one of the greatest joys of my life. During the 1914 war, she married a young and dashing cavalry officer in the French army. His name was Dupont — Charles Dupont — and they had a daughter. That child was baptised Christine, and I was her godfather. You are Christine, Carol.'

He paused, smiling at her. Her face was a picture of bewilderment, grave and troubled, but the deep brown eyes were steady as she looked at him. 'What happened then?' she said quietly.

'Dupont was killed in action, and shortly afterwards his wife died in a traffic accident in Paris. You were left alone in the world with only a young English nurse to look after you. She was a good woman, and deeply attached to you, though you were then no more than a few months old. Naturally I retained her services, and then she, too, married. Her husband's name was Marney; and after getting to know him well, I agreed to your legal adoption as their own child, my one stipulation being that I should remain completely in the background.'

'What was your object in doing that?' Her voice was gentle.

'I was engaged on dangerous work. At any time I might have come to a sticky end, and there seemed no need to expose you to sorrow and danger through my service to France.'

'I don't quite see what you mean,' she said in a puzzled tone. 'How could I have been in danger?'

'There were certain of my enemies who knew that I was very fond of you, my dear. There was always the risk that they would try to attack me through you. I considered it safer for you to remain in ignorance of your real birth and my relationship to you. Needless to say, I kept an eye on you right from the moment you left France with your new parents, and when it was impossible for me to do so, Gaston took my place. He it was who obtained a photograph of you one day. He became as enthusiastic for your well-being as I myself was.'

'Who exactly was Francois Gaston?' she asked quietly. 'He certainly didn't know me when we found him dying in York.'

'I think,' I put in gently, 'he was too far

gone to recognise anyone.'

Antoine ignored my interruption. 'He was Charles Dupont's step-brother, Carol, hence his interest in you. Strange character as he undoubtedly was, I have already said that his heart was big. Even if he was dying, I think he would prefer that you did not know him for what he was. I feel sure he must have known you in York, but being a strange man, refused to let you see it.'

She nodded, still somewhat bewildered. For my part, I was beginning to see things in their proper light, and the picture was a lot better than I had imagined. 'Where does this sapphire ring come into it?' I asked. I could contain my curiosity on that score no longer.

Antoine gave a delightful little chuckle. 'I thought that you would be asking that before I finished. Napoleon's ring was one of my most treasured possessions. It was something of a wrench when we included it in the stuff that was stolen in our first plan. Its very value, however, made it the ideal bait we needed, and I sacrificed it gladly. Gaston swore he would recover it, and in return I promised him that if he succeeded in doing so, I should be glad to fulfil his dearest wish.'

'What was that wish?' I asked.

'That Carol should have the ring.'

'I see,' I said. 'Everything seems quite clear and simple now, but believe me, it was a nightmare before. We didn't know where we were, or what was happening! In fact, I owe you an apology. At one time I actually thought you were one of the chief crooks!'

He laughed. 'It's not really surprising, I suppose. However, all's well that ends well, as you English say.'

I considered a moment before speaking. Then: 'In view of what you've told us, what are you proposing to do now?'

'Take you direct to your MI5,' he said quietly. 'They will handle the rest of the matter in their own way. My part is finished.'

'And mine.' I grinned as I pressed the starter.

'France will reward you, *mon ami*.' He smiled.

I looked across at Carol. Her eyes were

shining brightly as she met my gaze. 'France has already given me all I ever want,' I said softly.

We do hope that you have enjoyed reading this large print book.

Did you know that all of our titles are available for purchase?

We publish a wide range of high quality large print books including:
Romances, Mysteries, Classics
General Fiction
Non Fiction and Westerns

Special interest titles available in large print are:
The Little Oxford Dictionary
Music Book, Song Book
Hymn Book, Service Book

Also available from us courtesy of Oxford University Press:
Young Readers' Dictionary
(large print edition)
Young Readers' Thesaurus
(large print edition)

For further information or a free brochure, please contact us at:
Ulverscroft Large Print Books Ltd.,
The Green, Bradgate Road, Anstey,
Leicester, LE7 7FU, England.
Tel: (00 44) 0116 236 4325
Fax: (00 44) 0116 234 0205

Other titles in the
Linford Mystery Library:

WHO IS JACQUELINE?

Victor Rousseau

After following a lone husky on the street, Paul Hewlett encounters the dog's owner — a beautiful young woman in furs, who is then savagely set upon by two strangers who attempt to abduct her. Thanks to Paul and the faithful hound, the would-be kidnappers are repelled, and he takes the mysterious woman — Jacqueline — to his apartment, leaving her there to sleep. But on returning, he discovers a grisly tableau: Jacqueline clutching a blood-stained knife, with a dead man at her feet . . .

THE NIGHTMARE MURDERS

Gerald Verner

Following a strange compulsion, Robert Harcourt finds himself consulting a fortune teller who gives him a sinister message. He says he sees Robert in a mansion, surrounded by happy faces. There is a woman, a beautiful woman. Robert is attracted to her, but hurts her cruelly, and so deeply that she will never forgive him. That very night, as the clock strikes the hour of midnight, Robert will take the life of a man dear to her. He will become — *a murderer*!

THE TIPSTER

Gerald Verner

A mysterious man. calling himself 'the Tipster' telephones the *Daily Clarion* newspaper and announces his intention to commit five murders, beginning with Lord Latimer, Senior Steward of the Jockey Club. John Tully, News Editor of the *Daily Clarion*, believes the call to be a hoax by a madman — until Lord Latimer is shot dead while walking in the grounds of his house at Newbury. Superintendent Budd of Scotland Yard is called to investigate; but his powers are put to the test as several more people are brutally murdered . . .

THE MISSING SCHOOLGIRL

Shelley Smith

A schoolgirl goes missing after speaking to a strange man. A jilted painter sets out to take revenge on his rival in both love and art. A room to let harbours a macabre secret. A man fears his soul has been stolen. A woman is haunted by visions of a lost child. An antiques dealer happens across a crook who has previously defrauded him. A foster child has a peculiar obsession with an old painting . . . Seven stories of crime, fear, and the mysterious workings of the mind.

THE MISTRESS OF EVIL

V. J. Banis

John Hamilton travels to the Carpathian Mountains in Romania, along with his wife Victoria and her sister Carolyn, to research the risk of earthquakes in the area. The government provides lodgings for them in the ancient Castle Drakul. Upon investigating a disused basement room, the trio discover a skeleton in a coffin with a wooden stake through its rib cage — and Carolyn feels a strange compulsion to goad John into removing it. Soon afterward, a sinister visitor arrives at the castle — claiming to be a descendant of the original Count Drakul . . .

THE GREEN MANDARIN MYSTERY

Denis Hughes

When a number of eminent scientists — all experts in their field, and of inestimable value to the British Government — mysteriously vanish, the police are at their wits' end. The only clue in each instance is a note left by the scientist saying they have joined 'the Green Mandarin'. Desperate to locate his daughter, Fleurette, a Home Office official enlists the services of scientific detective Ray Ellis. But as his investigations get closer to the truth, will Ray be the next person to go missing?